ILLUSTRATED CLASSICS

Kidnapped

Robert Louis Stevenson

Adapted by
Lucy Collins

Edited by
Claire Black

Published by

Berryland
Books
www.berrylandbooks.com

Kidnapped

Robert Louis Stevenson

First Published in 2006 • Copyright © Berryland Books 2006
ISBN 1-84577-093-5 • Printed in India

Contents

I Set Off Upon My Journey

My adventures began on a morning in June, 1751, when I locked my father's house for the last time. The sun was shining upon the hills, and the blackbirds whistling among the garden flowers, as I went down the road. The mist that hung around the valley at dawn was beginning to die away.

Mr. Campbell, the minister of Essendean was

waiting for me at the garden gate.

"Well, Davie, have you had your breakfast?" he asked.

When I nodded in affirmative, he took my hand in both of his, and clapped it kindly under his arm.

"I will go with you as far as the ford, to set you on the way."

And then, we began to walk forward in silence.

"Are you sorry to leave the village of Essendean?" Mr. Campbell asked, after we had walked for some time.

"Why, sir," I asked, "since my father and mother are no more, I shall be no nearer to them in Essendean, than in any other place in this world. Moreover, if I get good work for myself where I am going, I would go willingly."

"Very well, Davie;" said Mr. Campbell, "so now it's time for me to tell you something important. When your mother was gone, and your father was on his deathbed, he gave me a letter, which he said was your inheritance.

'When I am gone,' your father told me, 'and the house is emptied and the things disposed of, give this letter to my boy, and send him off to the house of Shaws, not far from Cramond. That is the place I came from,' he had said, 'and it's proper that my boy should return there.'"

"The house of Shaws!" I cried. "What had my poor father to do with the Shaws?"

"Who can tell that for sure?" said Mr. Campbell. "But the name of that family, Davie, is the name you bear - Balfours of Shaws: a reputable, ancient and honest family, though these days the estate is somewhat decayed. Your father, too, was a man of learning as befitted his position; but his manners or speech was not that of a common school teacher."

And so saying, Mr. Campbell handed me a letter, which was addressed as follows:

"To the hands of Ebenezer Balfour, Esquire,

of Shaws,

These will be delivered by my son, David Balfour."

My heart was beating hard at this great prospect, which had so suddenly opened before a seventeen year old lad, the son of a poor country school teacher.

"Mr. Campbell," I stammered, "and if you were in my shoes, would you go?"

"Surely, I would," said the minister. "Two days of walking would take a young boy like you to Cramond, which is near Edinburgh. And even if it came to the worst and you were shown the door by your relations, you can always come back. However, I would hope, my boy that no such thing happens, and you would, in time, come to be a great man."

He then drew a picture of the great house that I was bound to, and told me how I should conduct myself there.

"Keep in mind that you have had a countryside

upbringing," said Mr. Campbell. "Don't shame us, Davie, with any country boy manners. In that great house, with all those servants, show yourself to be a quiet, polite and sensible young man."

"Sir," said I, "I promise you that I'll try to do so."

"Very well then," said Mr. Campbell, "I have here a little packet which contains four things. One is the money from the sale of your father's books and belongings; the other three is what Mrs. Campbell and I would like you to accept from us."

Mr. Campbell then embraced me, and held me at arm's length, looking at me with his face full of sadness. Then, bidding good-bye, he left me to be on my own.

I was now to go to a busy house, among rich and respected gentlefolk of my own name and blood.

On the second day of my journey, as I came atop a hill, I saw down below, in the midst of a long ridge, the city of Edinburgh smoking like a furnace.

Presently, I came by a house where a shepherd lived, and got the directions for the neighborhood of the village Cramond. As I went a little further I passed Glasgow Road, and soon, I was told that I was in Cramond parish.

Subsequently, I began asking the people I met on my way, the directions to the house of Shaws. But, the question surprised almost everybody. At first I thought that my dusty and travel worn appearance was very much unlike the greatness of the place to which I was bound; but after two or three people had given me the same look and the same answer, I began to wonder if there was something strange about the Shaws themselves.

Towards sundown, I met a dark, sour-looking woman who came trudging down a hill. When I repeated my question to her, she turned about sharp, accompanied me back to the hilltop she had just left, and pointed to a great bulk of building standing in the bottom of the next valley.

The house appeared to be a kind of ruin; no road led up to it, there was no garden, and no smoke arose from any of the chimneys. My heart sank. "That!" I cried.

The woman's face lit up with a spiteful anger. "That is the house of Shaws!" she cried back. "Blood built it; blood stopped the building of it; blood shall bring it down! I curse the house, and curse all those who stay or go into that house!"

And then, she turned with a skip, and was gone.

I stood where she left me, with my hair on end. In those days people still believed in witches and trembled at a curse; and the woman's curse took all the strength out of my legs. I sat and stared at the house of Shaws, unsure as to whether I should retreat or proceed.

At last, as the sun went down, I saw a scroll of smoke curling up from one of the chimneys. It was hardly thicker than the smoke arising from a candle. But, to me, it meant a fire and warmth, and more importantly, the proof that someone was living in there. So, I set forward along a little faint track in the grass that led towards the house.

Soon, I came upon stone pillars with an unroofed cabin beside them, and coats of arms upon the top. It was obviously supposed to be the main entrance, but was unfinished. Instead of iron gates, two stick frames were tied across with a straw rope.

The nearer I went, the drearier the house appeared. It seemed that one section of the house was never completed. Where the upper floors should have been, I could see only open steps and staircases, showing that the builders had left before completion. Many of the windows didn't have glass, and bats flew in and out.

The night had begun to fall as I approached the house; and in three of the lower windows, which were very high up, narrow, and well barred, the changing light of a little fire began to glimmer. I clearly remember how, in my father's house, the fire and the bright lights could be seen even a mile away! I began to wonder about the place I was going to. Was this the place where I was to seek new friends and great fortunes?

As I went forward cautiously, I could hear the rattling of dishes and a dry rasping cough. But there was no sound of speech and not even a dog barked.

With a throbbing heart, I knocked at the door. Then, I stood and waited.

The house had fallen into a dead silence; a whole minute passed, and nothing stirred but the bats overhead. I knocked again; but whoever was in that house kept deadly still.

I was in two minds whether to run away; but my anger got the better of me, and I began, instead, to rain kicks and punches on the door, and to shout out aloud for Mr. Balfour.

Suddenly, I could hear someone coughing right overhead. Looking up, I saw a man's head

in a tall nightcap, and the mouth of a shot-gun at one of the first storey windows.

"It's loaded," said a voice.

"I have come here with a letter," I said, "for Mr. Ebenezer Balfour of Shaws. Is he here?"

"Well, you can put it upon the doorstep and leave," was the reply.

"I will do no such thing," I cried, growing angry now. "It is a letter of introduction, and I will deliver it into Mr. Balfour's hands."

"Who are you, yourself?" was the next question, coming after a pause.

"I am David Balfour," said I.

I am sure that the man was shocked to hear that, for, I heard the gun barrel rattling on the window sill.

"Is your father dead?" he asked, after quite a long while.

I was so surprised at this, that I could find no voice to answer.

"He must be dead, no doubt," the man resumed. "And that'll be what brings you tapping to my door."

There was another pause, and then, "Well, man," he said, "I'll let you in."

And he disappeared from the window.

CHAPTER 2

I Meet My Uncle

There was a great rattling of chains and bolts, and the door was opened and shut again behind me as soon as I had passed.

"Go into the kitchen and touch nothing," said the voice from the shadows.

I groped my way forward and entered the kitchen.

The firelight showed me the barest room I

ever saw. Half-a-dozen dishes stood upon the shelves, the table was laid for supper with a bowl of porridge, a horn spoon, and a cup of beer. Apart from these, there was nothing in that vast stony chamber, except for a few padlocked chests and a cupboard.

As I was observing my surroundings, the man rejoined me. He was a mean, stooping, clay-faced creature; and his age might have been anything between fifty and seventy. He was wearing a flannel nightgown and nightcap, and had not shaved for a long time.

But what was particularly distressing to me was that neither did he take his eyes away from my face, nor did he dare to look straight in my face.

He seemed like an old servant, who had been left in charge of that big house.

"Are you hungry?" said he. "You can eat that porridge."

I said I feared it was his supper.

"O," said he, "I can do without it. I'll take the beer though, for it moistens my cough."

He drank some beer from the cup, still keeping an eye upon me as he drank. Then, suddenly, he held out his hand.

"Let's see the letter," he said.

I told him the letter was for Mr. Balfour, not for him.

"And who do you think I am?" he asked. "Give me Alexander's letter."

"You know my father's name?"

"It would be strange if I did not," he replied, "for he was my born brother and I'm your born uncle. So give us the letter."

If I were a few years younger, I surely would have burst into tears with humiliation and disappointment. Even now, I could find no words, but handed him the letter, and sat down to the porridge with little or no appetite.

Meanwhile, my uncle, stooping over the fire, turned the letter again and again in his hands.

"What brings you here?" he asked, suddenly.

"To give the letter," said I.

"No," he said, cunningly, "I mean what other hopes do you have?"

"I confess, sir," said I, "when I was told that I had relatives who were quite well-to-do, I hoped that they might help me in my life. But I am no beggar, and I look for no favors from you. For, though I might appear to be poor, I have friends who will be glad to help me."

"Hoot-toot!" said Uncle Ebenezer. "Don't fly out at a temper at me. We'll get along fine. And boy, if you're done with that porridge, I could just taste it myself."

The very next moment, he had driven me out of the chair and spoon, and had started digging into the porridge with gusto. Then he gulped down some beer, and said, "If you are thirsty, you'll find water behind the door."

I didn't make any answer to this, but stood looking at my uncle with an angry heart. He, meanwhile, continued to eat hurriedly, and to throw out little darting glances at me. Once, when our eyes met, he looked guiltier than a thief who had been caught with his hand in a man's pocket.

I was awakened from these thoughts by his sharp voice.

"Did your father die a long time back?" he asked.

"Three weeks ago, sir," said I.

"Alexander was a silent, secretive man," he said. "He never spoke much when he was young. He never spoke of me, did he?"

"I never knew he had a brother till you told me," I replied.

"Dear me, dear me!" said Uncle Ebenezer. "Nothing about the Shaws as well, I dare say?"

"No, sir," I replied.

My uncle seemed quite satisfied to hear that. Before long, he jumped up, came towards me, and whacked me upon my shoulder.

"I'm just glad I let you in," said he. "And now, I will take you to your bed."

To my surprise, he didn't light any lamp, but set forward into the dark passage. I stumbled after him in the darkness.

Finally, he paused before a room and bade me in.

I begged for a light to go to bed with.

"Hoot-toot!" said Uncle Ebenezer. "There's a fine moon tonight."

"But, it's so dark that I cannot see the bed," I protested.

"Hoot-toot!" said he. "I do not agree with having lights in a house. I'm afraid of fires."

Then, before I could utter a word, he bade me good-night and went out; and I heard him lock me in from the outside.

The room was as cold as a well, and the bed, as damp as a mud-bed. But luckily I had caught up my bundle and woolen cloth. So, rolling myself in, I lay down upon the floor and soon fell asleep.

In the morning, I opened my eyes to find myself in a great room furnished with fine embroidered furniture. Ten or twenty years ago, it must have been a pleasant enough room; but damp, dirt, disuse, and the mice had ruined it.

Meanwhile, I could see the sun shining outside through the windows; and being very cold in that miserable room, I knocked and shouted till my uncle came and let me out. He led me to the back of the house, to a draw-well, and told me to "wash my face."

When that was done, I made my way back to the kitchen where the table was laid with two bowls of porridge but only one cup of beer.

Perhaps my uncle saw me staring in surprise at the single cup, for, he asked me whether I would like some beer.

I told him yes, but that he should not trouble himself about it.

"No, no," said he, "I wouldn't deny you anything reasonable."

Then, to my great surprise, he took out another small cup, and carefully poured half the beer from one cup to the other.

I was now convinced that my uncle was indeed a great miser.

At the end of our meal, my uncle sat down in the sun at one of the windows. He asked me several questions.

Once it was, "And your mother?"

I told him that she, too, was dead.

"Oh, she was a pretty girl."

Then, after a long pause, "Who were those friends of yours you so dearly spoke of?"

I told him that his name was Campbell.

"Davie, my man," said he, "you've come to the right place. I've a great notion of the family, and I want to do what's right by you; but it's going to take me some time to decide what occupation is right for you - the law, or the ministry, or maybe the army – but, in the meantime, I want you to keep your tongue within your teeth. No letters;

no messages; no kind of word to anybody; or else – there's my door."

"Uncle Ebenezer," said I, "I've no reason to suppose you mean well by me. I want you to know that I have a pride of my own and if you show me your door again, I'll leave instantly."

"Hoots-toots," said he, "I didn't mean that. What's mine is yours, Davie, and what's yours is mine. Blood's thicker than water; and there's nobody but you and me in our family."

"But now, I have to go and meet the session clerk," he added, and then opening a chest, he took out a very old, well-preserved blue coat and a good hat. These he wore, and was about to go out, when a thought arrested him.

"I cannot leave you by yourself in the house," said he. "I'll have to lock you out."

The blood came to my face.

"If you lock me out," said I, "it'll be the last you'll see of me in friendship."

"Well, well," said he, "we must bear and

forbear. I'll not go."

"Uncle Ebenezer," I said, "I can make nothing out of this. You treat me like a thief; you hate to have me in this house; you let me see it. It's not possible that you can like me. Why do you want to keep me, then? Let me go back to the friends I have!"

"Na," he said, very earnestly. "I quite like you; and for the honor of the family I couldn't let you return. Soon, you'll find that we agree with each other."

"Well, sir," said I, after I had thought for some time, "I'll stay awhile. And if we don't agree, it shall not be because of any fault of mine."

CHAPTER 3

I Run A Great Danger

For a day that had begun so ill, the rest of it passed fairly well.

We had more porridge for lunch. In the afternoon, I took great pleasure in reading some books which I found in the room next to the kitchen. There were a large number of both English and Latin books in the room.

One thing which I discovered put me in some

doubt. On the first page of one of the books, the following words were written:

"To my brother Ebenezer on his fifth birthday."

And the handwriting was my father's.

Now, what puzzled me was: as Uncle Ebenezer had inherited the family house, my father was surely the younger brother. And that meant my father had either made some error while writing, or he had written this before he was even five years old!

Puzzled, I went back into the kitchen and sat down to porridge. The first thing I said to Uncle Ebenezer was to ask him if my father had been very bright at his studies.

"Alexander? Not he!" was the reply. "I was far quicker myself when I was young. Why, I could read as soon as he could."

This puzzled me even more! So, I asked if he and my father had been twins.

Hearing this, Uncle Ebenezer jumped upon

his stool, and the spoon fell out of his hand upon the floor.

"Why are you asking that?" he shouted, and he caught me by the breast of the jacket. His eyes were flashing strangely.

"What do you mean?" I asked, very calmly, for I was far stronger than him.

"Take your hand from my jacket. This is no way to behave."

My uncle made a great effort to calm himself down.

"David," he said, "you should not speak to me about your father. He was the only brother that ever I had, and talking about him upsets me."

And then, he caught up his spoon and fell to supper again.

After some time, he broke the silence by telling me of a promise he had made to my father before my birth.

"I'd promised Alexander that I would put a little money aside for you," he explained. "It was nothing legal, just a gentleman's promise. And the money has grown by now to be… just exactly…" here, my uncle paused and stumbled -- "of just exactly forty pounds!"

I could see that the whole story was a lie, invented with some purpose which I couldn't guess at.

I said, in a mocking tone, "O, really, sir! It's in pounds sterling I think!"

"Yes, indeed," returned my uncle; "and if you'll step out a minute, I'll get the money out, and call you in again."

I did so; and after a while, was called inside again.

My uncle counted out thirty seven gold coins into my hand; the rest was in his hand, in small gold and silver. But, there his greedy heart failed him, and he shoved the change into his pocket.

Now, my uncle seemed so miserly that I was dumbstruck by this sudden generosity, and could find no words with which to thank him. However,

I kept wondering all the while, what would come next.

And soon enough, the old man asked for a return favor.

I waited for something monstrous to come my way; but, the request was reasonable -- he asked for help around the house.

I told him that I was ready and willing to help him.

"Well," he said, "let's begin." He pulled out a rusty key from his pocket. "This is the key to the stair-tower at the far end of the house. You can only enter it from the outside, for that part of the house is unfinished. Go in there, and up the stairs, and bring me down the chest that's at the top. There are papers in it." he said.

"Can I have a light, sir?" I asked.

"No," he said. "No lights in my house."

"Very well, sir," said I. "Are the stairs good?"

"They're grand," said he; and then he added, "There are no banisters, so keep to the wall."

So, I went out into the night.

The wind was still moaning in the distance, though it was all quiet near the house of Shaws. It was now darker than ever; and I had to feel my way along the wall, till at last, I reached the stair-tower door.

I had got the key into the keyhole and had just turned it, when suddenly the whole sky lighted up with wild fire and went black again. I had to put my hand over my eyes to get back to the color of the darkness; and indeed I was already half blinded when I stepped into the tower.

It was so dark inside, that I had to feel about for the wall with one hand, and the lowermost step of the stair with the other. Minding my uncle's word about the banisters, I kept close to the wall, and felt my way in the pitch darkness with a beating heart.

The house of Shaws stood some five full storeys high, and as I advanced, it seemed to me the stair grew airier and a bit brighter; and I was wondering what might be the cause of this change, when a second flash of the lightning came and went.

I did not cry out because fear had choked my throat.

Not only did the lightning shine in on every side through huge cracks in the wall, so that seemed to be climbing up upon an open scaffold the same lightning also showed me that the step were of unequal length, and that one of my fee rested that moment within two inches of the pit.

'So, this was the grand stair!' I thought; and a sort of angry courage came into my heart. My uncle had sent me here, certainly to run great risks, or perhaps to die. I swore that I would finish the job, even if I should break my neck for it.

I got down on my hands and knees; and as slowly as a snail, feeling before me every inch, and testing the solidity of every stone, I continued to climb the stair.

I felt for the door of the tower, unlocked it, and stumbled inside feeling for the solid grand staircase. I started climbing. The darkness appeared to have redoubled now. Moreover, I was now troubled by a great swarm of bats that flew downwards from the top of the tower, sometimes beating about my face and body.

However, I continued to climb up on hands and knees. As I turned a corner of the tower, suddenly, my hand slipped upon an edge and found nothing but emptiness beyond it. The stairs, unfinished, had totally ended! So, my uncle had indeed sent me to die!!

I turned and fumbled my way down again, with a great anger in my heart.

When I was half-way down, it started raining heavily. I put out my head into the storm, and looked along towards the kitchen. I thought I could see a figure standing, quite still, like a man listening carefully. And then there came a blinding flash, which showed me my uncle plainly, and then followed a great clap of thunder.

I am not sure whether my uncle thought the crash to be the sound of my fall, but he was seized by a fit of panic and ran into the house. I too followed him silently inside.

There, I saw my uncle sitting with his back towards me at the table. Now and again he would start shuddering and groaning aloud.

I stepped behind him, and clapped my hand on his shoulder.

My uncle gave a kind of broken cry like a

sheep's bleat, flung up his arms, and tumbled to the floor like a dead man. I was somewhat shocked at this; but I had to arm myself first of all, and did not hesitate to let him lie as he had fallen. I quickly took the keys and looked through his cabinets. I found a rusty, ugly-looking Highland dirk without the scabbard. This, then, I concealed inside my waistcoat, and turned to my uncle.

He was lying still. So, I splashed water on his face. When he came back to his senses, he looked at me and a sort of fear came into his eyes.

"Are you alive?" he sobbed. "O, are you alive?"

"That I am," said I. "Small thanks to you!"

He had begun to seek for his breath with deep sighs.

"The blue phial," said he, "...in the cupboard – the blue phial."

I ran to the cupboard, and, found there a blue phial of medicine, and this I administered to him.

"It's the trouble," said my uncle, reviving a little;

"I have a trouble, Davie. It's the heart."

I set him on a chair.

It is true I felt some pity for him, but I was full of anger and had a number of explanations to ask of my uncle.

I asked him why he tried to kill me.

"I'll tell you in the morning," he said, "as sure as death I will."

And so weak was he that I could do nothing but consent. I locked him into his room, and then returning to the kitchen, I wrapped myself in my woolen cloth, lay down upon the chests and fell asleep.

CHAPTER 4

I Go To The Queen's Ferry

I had no doubt now about my uncle's enmity and that he would leave no stone unturned to destroy me. But I was young and spirited, and had a great opinion of my craftiness. I was sure I could foil all his treacherous schemes.

I sat there smiling, and imagined myself finding out his secrets one after another, and in time, growing to be that man's king and ruler.

Next, I went upstairs and gave my prisoner his liberty.

Soon, we were sitting at our breakfast, as it might have been the day before.

"Well, sir" said I, "have you nothing more to say to me?"

And then, as he made no reply, I continued, "Why did you cheat me and attempt to kill me…"

At this moment, we were interrupted by a knocking at the door.

Bidding my uncle sit where he was, I went to open it, and found on the doorstep, a half-grown boy in sea-clothes. He was blue with the cold.

"I've brought a letter for Mr. Belflower from old Heasyoasy," he said, with a cracked voice. "And I say, mate," he added, "I'm terribly hungry."

"Well," I said, "come into the house, and have a bite."

I brought him in and set him down at my own place. The poor chap fell-to greedily on the remains of the breakfast. Meanwhile, my uncle had read the letter and sat thinking. Then, suddenly, he got to his feet, and pulled me apart.

"Davie," said my uncle, "I have a business with Hoseason, the captain of a trading ship - the Covenant. Now, if you and me walk over with this lad, I could see the captain in town, or maybe on board the Covenant if there were any papers to be signed; and then we can go to the lawyer, Mr. Rankeillor's. After what has passed, you would be unwilling to believe me; but, you'll believe Rankeillor. He's a highly respected man in these parts and besides, he knew your father."

I stood thinking for some time. I was going to some place of shipping, which undoubtedly would have a lot of people around; and there my uncle would not dare to attempt any violence. Once there, I believed I could force on the visit to the lawyer. Besides, as I had lived in inland hills all my life, I was intrigued by the very thought of being able to have a closer look at the sailing ships.

"Very well," I said, "let us go to the Ferry."

So, we locked the door and set forth upon our walk.

On the way, the cabin-boy told me his name was Ransome. He had been at the sea since he was nine, but he wasn't sure of his present age as he had lost track of the years. I asked Ransome about the ship and about Captain Hoseason, in whose praises he was loud.

Heasyoasy (as Ransome called Captain Hoseason), according to him, was a rough, fierce, and brutal man; and all this my poor cabin-boy had taught himself to admire, as it was very seamanlike and manly. Ransome would only admit one flaw in his idol.

"He is no seaman," he admitted. "It is Mr. Shuan who navigates the ship; he's the finest seaman in the trade, except for his love of drink. Why, look here;" and turning down his stocking he showed me a raw red wound that made my blood run cold.

"He done that -- Mr. Shuan done it," he said, with an air of pride.

"What!" I cried, "Do you put up with such savage usage? Why, you are no slave to be handled like that!"

"No," said Ransome, changing his tune at once, "and so he'll find. See here;" and he showed me a great case-knife, which he told me was stolen.

"O," he cried, "let me see him try that again; I dare him to; I'll do for him! O, he is not the first one!"

And he confirmed it with a poor, silly, ugly oath.

I have never felt such pity for any one in this wide world as I felt for Ransome.

The boy told me further, that there were criminals being carried across the sea to slavery in North America and young children were kidnapped for private interest or revenge. Although Ransome seemed to quite enjoy this life, I could make out how horribly they treated him.

At that point, we came on a hilltop from where we could see the Covenant, and the town of Queensferry in the distance. There was a pre-voyage bustle on board the ship; and I could hear the song of the sailors as they pulled upon the ropes.

After all I had listened to on the way, I looked at that ship with extreme loathing and pitied all the poor souls that were condemned to sail in her.

I told uncle Ebenezer that I would not step on board the ship, to which he agreed.

We came down the hill, and reached the Hawes inn, at the end of the dock. Ransome led us to a small room heated by a great fire of coal, with a bed in it. At a table, a tall, dark, sober-looking man sat writing.

I never saw any man look cooler or more studious and poised than this ship captain.

He got to his feet and offered his large hand

to Ebenezer.

"I am proud to see you, Mr. Balfour," said he, "and glad that you are here in time."

Though I had promised myself not to let uncle Ebenezer out of sight, I was impatient for a nearer look of the sea; and so, when the captain told me to 'run down-stairs and amuse myself awhile,' I was foolish enough to do so.

Crossing the road in front of the inn, I walked down upon the beach.

I looked at the seamen with the boats. They were big brown fellows, some in shirts, some with jackets, and all with their case-knives. I talked to one of these fellows, but on hearing all the terrible oaths which accompanied his conversation, I hastily got away from him.

Then I returned to Ransome; and shortly we were seated at a table in the front room of the inn, both eating and drinking.

Here it occurred to me that, as the landlord was a man of that province, I might do well to make a friend of him. So, I asked him if he knew Mr. Rankeillor. "Of course, I know him; he is a very honest man," he replied.

I said it seemed that Ebenezer was ill-seen in the country.

"No doubt," said the landlord. "He's a wicked old man, and there are many who would like to see him hanging by the rope. But, once he was a fine young fellow. That was before the rumor went round that he had killed his brother, Mr. Alexander."

"And what would he kill him for?" I asked.

"And what for, but just to get the place," said he.

"You mean the Shaws' place? Was Alexander the eldest son?" I asked him.

"Indeed he was," he replied.

And with that he went away.

I had guessed it a long while ago; and now I sat stunned with my good fortune. I could hardly believe that the same poor boy, who had trudged in the dust from Ettrick Forest, not two days ago, had a house and broad lands!

All these pleasant things, and a thousand others crowded into my mind as I sat staring before me out of the inn window. I only remember seeing Captain Hoseason down on the dock among his seamen.

Next, I heard my uncle calling me, and found the pair on the road together. It was the captain who addressed me.

"Sir," said he, "Mr. Balfour tells me great things about you. I wish I was here for a little more time, so that we could have more time to make better friends; but we'll make the most of what we have. I invite you aboard my ship for half an hour, and drink a bowl with me."

Although I was longing to see what the ship looked like on the inside, I told him that my uncle and I had an appointment with a lawyer.

"Yes," said the captain, "he told me about that. But, you see, the boat will set you ashore at the town dock, and that's very near to Rankeillor's house."

And here, the captain suddenly leaned down and whispered in my ear, "Beware of the old man; he means mischief. Come aboard so that we can talk in private."

And passing his arm through mine, he set off towards the boat. Soon, we were there, and the captain was helping me in the boat. When we were all set in our places, the boat was thrust off from the dock and began to move. I thought that I had found a good friend in the captain and rejoiced to see the ship.

As soon as we were alongside, Hoseason declared that he and I must be the first ones aboard. And so, I was helped onto the ship and set down again on the deck. There the captain stood ready waiting for me, and instantly slipped back his arm under mine. There I stood some while, a little dizzy with the unsteadiness of the ship, and yet vastly pleased with the strange sights. The captain, meanwhile, was pointing out the strangest articles, and telling me their names and uses.

"But where is my uncle?" I enquired, suddenly.

"Yes," said Hoseason, with a sudden grimness, "that's the point."

I felt I was lost. With all my strength, I plucked myself clear of Hoseason and ran to the bulwarks. Sure enough, there was the boat pulling for the town, with my uncle sitting in the stern. I gave a piercing cry, "Help, help!" and both sides of the anchorage rang with it. My uncle turned around, and showed me a face full of cruelty and terror.

It was the last I saw. Already strong hands had been plucking me back from the ship's side; and now a thunderbolt seemed to strike me; I saw a great flash of fire, and fell senseless.

CHAPTER 5

I Go To Sea In The "Covenant"

When I regained consciousness I found myself in darkness, in great pain, bound hand and foot and deafened by unfamiliar noises. As I realized that I must be lying somewhere in the belly of that unlucky ship, a blackness of despair fell upon me that once again robbed me of my senses.

I was awakened by the light of a hand-lantern

shining in my face. A small man of about thirty, with green eyes and a tangle of fair hair stood looking down at me.

"Well," said he, "how goes it?"

I answered by a sob; and my visitor then felt my pulse and set to dress the wound upon my scalp.

"A sore dunt (stroke)," he remarked, "What, man? Cheer up! Everything will be fine."

Then he gave me some brandy and water, and left me to myself.

The next time, the man with the green eyes came with the captain. The former examined me, and dressed my wound as before, while Hoseason looked me in my face with an odd, black look.

"Now, sir, you see for yourself," said the other man, "a high fever and no appetite."

"I am no magician, Mr. Riach," said the captain.

"Allow me, sir," said Riach; "I want that boy

taken out of this hole and put in the forecastle."

"What you may want sir, is a matter of concern to nobody but yourself," returned the captain, in a sharp voice; "but I can tell you he shall remain here only."

And Hoseason set one foot upon the ladder.

But Mr. Riach caught him by the sleeve.

"Admitting that you have been paid to do a murder..." he began.

Hoseason turned upon him with a flash.

"What's that?" he cried. "What kind of talk is that?"

"It seems it is the talk that you can understand," said Mr. Riach, looking steadily in Hoseason's face.

"Mr. Riach, I have sailed with you three cruises," replied the captain. "In all that time, sir, you should have learned to know me. If you say the lad will die…"

"Yes he will!" said Mr. Riach.

"Well, then put him where you please!" said Hoseason.

Five minutes later, my bonds were cut and I was carried up to the forecastle, and laid in a bunk on some sea-blankets.

The forecastle was a roomy place, set all about with berths in which the men off duty were seated, smoking or lying down asleep. One of these men brought me a drink of something healing which Mr. Riach had prepared.

Here I lay for many days, and not only got my health again, but came to know my companions. They were a rough lot indeed, as sailors mostly are: being men condemned to toss together on the rough seas, with masters no less cruel.

They were rough, sure enough; and bad, I suppose; but they had many virtues. They had traits of kindness and simplicity in them, and some sparks of honesty.

Among other good deeds that they did, they returned my money, which had been shared among them. And though it was about a third short, I was very glad to get it, and hoped great good from it in the land I was going to. The ship was bound for the Carolinas, and you mustn't suppose that I was merely exiled there. For those were the days when white men were still sold into slavery on the plantations, and that was the destiny to which my wicked uncle had condemned me.

All this time, the Covenant was tumbling up

and down against sea waves. All hands had to work continuously. The cabin-boy Ransome came in at times from the round-house where he served, now nursing a bruised limb in silent agony, now raving against the cruelty of Mr. Shuan, the chief mate.

It made my heart bleed; but the men had a great respect for the chief mate, who was, as they said, "the only seaman of the whole lot, and not such a bad man when he was sober." Indeed, I found there was a strange peculiarity about our two mates: that Mr. Riach was sullen, unkind, and harsh when he was sober, and Mr. Shuan would not hurt a fly except when he was drinking. I asked about the captain; but I was told drink made no difference upon that man of iron.

Meanwhile, I stayed as a prisoner and was never allowed to set my foot on deck.

CHAPTER 6

The Round-House

One night, a man of Mr. Riach's watch came below for his jacket; and a whisper began to go about the forecastle, "Shuan has done it at last."

Suddenly, the scuttle was flung open, and Captain Hoseason came down and addressed me. "My man," said he, "we want you to serve in the round-house. You and Ransome are to change berths."

Even as he spoke, two seamen appeared in the scuttle, carrying Ransome in their arms. At that very moment, the ship gave a great sheer into the sea, swinging the lantern, and the light fell directly on Ransome's face. It was as white as wax and had a look upon it like a dreadful smile. He neither spoke nor moved.

The blood ran cold in me.

"You there, away from here!" shouted Hoseason.

At once, I ran up the ladder on deck. The round-house, for which I was bound, and where I was now to sleep and serve, stood some six feet above the decks. Inside were a fixed table and bench; and two berths - one for the captain, and one for the two mates to share.

Underneath there was a store-room. All the best meat and drink in the ship were stored there. And all the firearms were set in a shelf in the round-house wall.

When I entered, Mr. Shuan was sitting at the table, with the brandy bottle in front of him. He was a tall man, strongly made and very black. He took no notice of my coming in; nor did he move when the captain followed and leant on the berth beside me.

Presently, Mr. Riach came in and gave the captain a glance that said the boy was dead, as plain as speaking. All three of us stood without a word, staring down at Mr. Shuan.

All of a sudden, he put out his hand to take the bottle. At that, Mr. Riach started forward and took it away from him, crying out, with an oath that there had been too much of this work, and that a judgment would fall upon the ship. And then he flung away the bottle into the sea.

Mr. Shuan was on his feet in a flash; he looked dazed, and would've harmed Mr. Riach, had not the captain stepped in.

"Sit down!" roared the captain. "Do you know what you've done? You've murdered the boy!"

Mr. Shuan sat down again, and put up his hand to his brow. "Well," he said, "he brought me a dirty cup!" At that word, the captain and I and Mr. Riach all looked at each other with a kind of frightened look; and then Hoseason walked up to his chief officer, bade him lie down and go to sleep.

"Ah!" cried Mr. Riach, "You should have interfered long ago. It's too late now."

"Mr. Riach," said the captain, "this must never

53

be known in Dysart. The boy went overboard, sir; that's the story we will tell the people." This was the first night of my duties.

From now on, I had to serve at the meals, and at night I was given a hard and cold bed to sleep on. And yet, in other ways it was an easy service. And as for Mr. Shuan, the drink or his crime had certainly troubled his mind. I cannot say that I ever saw him in his proper wits, and moreover, I was pretty sure that he had no clear idea of what he had done.

Altogether, it was not a very hard life for the time it lasted. I was as well fed as the best of them. Mr. Riach, who had been to the college, spoke to me like a friend, and told me many curious things.

But the shadow of poor Ransome lay on all four of us, and on me and Mr. Shuan, most heavily. And then I had another trouble of my own: I could picture myself slaving in the tobacco fields in the near future. This thought terrified me.

CHAPTER 7

The Man with the Belt of Gold

More than a week of terrible weather passed and the officers decided to follow the winds further south.

One night, I was serving Mr. Riach and the captain at their supper, when the ship struck something with a great sound. My two masters leaped to their feet.

"She's struck!" said Mr. Riach.

"No, sir," said the captain. "We've only run a boat down."

And it was actually so. We had run down a boat in the fog, and she had split in the midst and gone to the bottom. All her crew, but one had drowned.

When the captain brought the lone survivor into the round-house, and I set eyes on him for the first time, he looked as cool as I did. He was smallish in stature, but well set; he was sunburnt very dark, and heavily freckled and pitted with the small-pox. When he took off his great-coat, he laid a pair of fine silvermounted pistols on the table, and I saw that he was belted with a great sword. His manners were elegant.

Altogether I thought him to be a man I would rather call my friend than my enemy.

"I'm sorry, sir, about the boat," said the captain.

"There were some good men in it," said the stranger, "and I would rather see them on the dry land again, than ten such boats."

"Friends of yours?" said Hoseason.

"You don't have such friends in your country," was the reply. "They would have died for my sake."

"You've a French soldier's coat upon your back and a Scotch tongue in your head, to be sure," said the captain, (implying that he could tell from his French coat that he was a Jacobite, and thus not loyal to King George.)

"So?" said the stranger, "are you of the honest party?" (meaning, was he a Jacobite?)

"Why, sir," replied the captain, "I am a true Protestant and I thank God for it. Still, I can be sorry to see another man with his back to the wall."

"Can you so, indeed?" asked the Jacobite. "Well, sir, I would speak quite plainly to you. I was bound for France; and there was a French ship cruising here to pick me up; but she gave us the go-by in the fog. If you can set me ashore where

I was going, I promise to reward you highly for your trouble."

"In France?" said the captain. "No sir; that I cannot do. But where do you come from? We might talk of that."

And then the captain observed me standing in my corner, and packed me off to get supper for the gentleman.

I did my job swiftly, and when I came back into the round-house, I found the stranger had taken a money-belt from about his waist, and poured out a guinea or two upon the table. The captain was looking at the guineas, and then at the belt; and I thought he seemed excited.

"Give me half of it," he cried, "and I'll do the job!"

The stranger swept back the guineas into the belt, and put it on again under his waistcoat.

"I have told you, sir" said he, "that not one of it belongs to me. It belongs to my chief. I'll give you thirty guineas if you set me on the sea-shore or sixty if you set me on the Linnhe Loch. Take it, if you will; if not, you can do your worst."

"And if I give you over to the soldiers?" said Hoseason.

To this, the stranger explained that betraying him to the red coats would result in no money for Hoseason. The money was part of a rent which King George was looking for from the stranger's chief.

Consequently, the captain agreed on sixty guineas.

Once Hoseason left, I asked if the stranger was a Jacobite; to which he said,

"Yes."

Then, he sent me to Hoseason for the key to the liquor cabinet as he wanted some.

When I went there, I heard Mr. Riach, crying out, "Couldn't we trick him out of the round-house?"

"Hut!" said Hoseason. "We will start talking to the man, and then pin him by the two arms; or,

we can rush at him from both the doors and grab him before he has the time to draw his sword."

Hearing this, I was seized with both fear and anger at these treacherous, bloody men that I sailed with. My first thought was to run away, my second, was a bit bolder.

"Captain," said I, "the gentleman wants some liquor. Will you give me the key?"

They started and turned about.

"Why, here's our chance to get the firearms!" Riach cried, and then turned to me. "Listen you, David," said he, "do you know where the pistols are?"

"Yes," put in Hoseason. "David knows. You see, David my man, that wild highland man is a danger to the ship, besides being a rank enemy to King George, God bless him!"

"The trouble is," resumed the captain, "that all our firearms are in the roundhouse under this man's nose. Now, if any of the officers was to go in and take them, he would grow suspicious. But a lad like you, David, might snap up a pistol or two without remark. And if you can do it cleverly, I'll bear it in mind to make it good for you when we come to Carolina."

Here, Mr. Riach whispered to him a little.

"Very right, sir," said the captain; and then turned to myself, "And David, that man has a belt full of gold, and I give you my word that you shall have your share in it."

I told him I would do as he wished.

Upon that, he gave me the key of the spirit locker, and I began to go back to the round-house.

What was I to do? They were murderers and thieves, who had stolen me from my own country and killed poor Ransome. And was I to help them commit another murder? But, on the other hand, there was the fear of death; for what could a boy and a man do against a whole ship's company?

I was still in confusion, when I came into the round-house and saw the Jacobite eating his supper. All at once, my mind was made up. I walked right up to the table and put my hand on his shoulder.

"Do you want to be killed?" said I.

The man sprang to his feet, and looked questioningly at me.

"O!" cried I, "they're all murderers here; a ship full of them! They've murdered a boy already.

Now it's you."

"Yes," said he; "but they haven't got me yet."

Then he looked at me curiously, and said, "Will you stand with me?"

"Yes," said I. "I'll stand by you."

"Why, then," said he, "what's your name?"

"David Balfour," said I; and then, thinking that a man with so fine a coat must like fine people, I added for the first time, "of Shaws."

It never occurred to him to doubt me, for a Highlander is used to seeing great gentlefolk in great poverty.

"My name is Stewart," he said, drawing himself up. "Alan Breck, they call me."

Then, we turned our attention to preparing for the ambush. First, we checked the entrances to the round-house. The round-house was built very strong. Of its five openings, only the window on the ceiling and the two doors were large enough for the passage of a man. One was already shut and secured, and when I was proceeding to shut the other, Alan stopped me.

"It would be better if we shut it," I said.

"Not so, David," said he. "You see, I have but one face; but so long as that door is open and my face to it, the best part of my enemies will be in front of me." Then he gave me from the rack a cutlass, and next, he set me down to the table with a powder-horn, a bag of bullets and all the pistols, which he bade me charge.

"Now," said he, "how many are against us?"

I counted them up.

"Fifteen," said I.

"Well, it can't be helped," said he. "Now follow me. I'll keep this door, where I look for the main battle." "But, sir" said I, "what if they break in the door behind you?"

"That is a part of your work," said he. "As soon as the pistols are fired, you climb up into that bed where you'd be handy at the window. And if they lift hand against the door, you're to shoot at once."

CHAPTER 8

The Siege of the Round-House

Those on deck had waited for me till they grew impatient; and just as Alan had stopped speaking, the captain appeared at the open door.

"Stand!" cried Alan, and pointed his sword at him.

The captain stood; but he neither winced nor drew back a foot.

"A naked sword?!" he exclaimed. "This is a

strange return for hospitality."

"Do you see my sword?" said Alan. "The sooner the clash begins, the sooner you'll taste this steel throughout your vitals."

The captain said nothing to Alan, but he looked at me with an ugly look.

"David," said he, "I'll remember this."

The next moment, he was gone.

Alan alerted me that the ambush of men might come any minute.

A little while later, there was a rush of feet and a roar, and the men entered the room.

I saw Mr. Shuan attacking Alan directly. "That's him that killed the boy!" I cried.

I saw Alan giving him a killing blow.

Meanwhile, five men rushed past me trying to push the door in, forcing me to shoot a pistol for the first time ever in my life.

My first shot injured one man, possibly the captain. The next two shots were fired wide but scared the group of men back onto the deck.

The whole place was full of the smoke of my own firing.

As the smoke cleared, I saw Alan, standing as before; only now his sword was running blood to the hilt, and he was so swollen with triumph that he looked quite invincible.

He asked me if I had done much execution.

I told him I had hurt one, and thought it was the captain.

Alan told me to expect more attacks. So, I settled back to my place and kept watch. Our enemies were disputing not far off upon the deck.

"Unless we can crush them properly," said Alan, "there'll be no sleep for either you or me. But this time, mind, they'll be in earnest."

My pistols were ready. Soon, I began to hear stealthy steps and a brushing of men's clothes against the round-house wall, and knew they were taking their places. All this was upon Alan's side; and I had begun to think my share of the fight was at an end, when I heard someone drop softly on the roof above me.

A knot of them, cutlass in hand, made a rush against the door; and at the same moment, the glass of the window was dashed in a thousand pieces, and a man landed on the floor. Before he got his feet, I had clapped a pistol to his back. But I couldn't bring myself to fire at him.

Meanwhile, when the man felt the pistol, he whipped straight round and laid hold of me; and at that, I gave a shriek and shot him.

Then I saw a second fellow trying to drop in through the window. I shot him through the thigh, so that he slipped and tumbled on his companion's body.

Alan had kept the door for long; but one of the seamen had run in under his guard and gripped him. Another had broken in and had his cutlass ready. The door was crowded with faces. I was still thinking we were lost, when lo! Alan overpowered the wrestler, and charged at the others. The sword in his hands flashed like quicksilver; and at every flash there came the scream of a man hurt. Alan was driving the enemy along the deck as a sheep-dog chases sheep.

Yet, being very cautious Alan was soon back again.

The round-house was like a shambles; three were dead inside, another lay dying across the threshold.

Alan came up to me with open arms. "Come to my arms!" he cried, and embraced and kissed me on both cheeks. "David," said he, "I love you like a brother. And O man, am I not a bonny fighter?"

But, my heart was heavy; the thought of the two men I had shot was like a nightmare; and all of a sudden, I began to cry like a child.

Alan clapped my shoulder, and said I was a brave lad and wanted nothing but a sleep.

"I'll take the first watch," said he. "You've been with me, David, first and last; and I wouldn't lose you for anything."

So he took the first watch, pistol in hand and sword on knee for three hours. Then he roused me up, and I took my turn of three hours. Then, it was broad daylight, and a very quiet morning. The smooth, rolling sea tossed the ship, and a heavy rain drummed upon the roof. Throughout my watch nothing stirred; and by the banging of the helm, I knew they had even no one at the tiller. I learned afterwards so many of them were hurt or dead, and the rest in so ill a temper, that Mr. Riach and the captain had to take turn and turn like Alan and me, or the ship might have gone ashore and nobody would have known.

Meanwhile, the sound of birds informed me that we were near land.

Alan and I sat down to breakfast at about 6 o' clock. We had at our command all the drink in the ship and all the dainty food. However, the floor was covered with broken glass and was in a horrid mess of blood, which took away my appetite.

Alan and I made a good company for each other, and Alan cut off one of the silver buttons from his coat, and gave it to me as a gift of gratitude.

"I had them from my father," he said, "now I give one to you. Wherever you go and show that button, the friends of Alan Breck will come around you."

At this moment, we were hailed by Mr. Riach from the deck, asking for a parley. I climbed through the window, and sitting on the edge of it, pistol in hand, hailed him back again and bade him speak out. He came to the edge of the round-house and we looked at each other in silence for a while.

"This is a bad job," said he at last.

"We didn't choose it," said I.

"The captain," he said, "would like to speak with your friend."

Thereupon I consulted with Alan, and the parley was agreed to and parole given upon either side.

A little after, the captain came to one of the windows, looking pale. Alan at once held a pistol in his face.

"Put that thing up!" said the captain. "Have I not given my word, sir?"

"Captain," said Alan, "you had given me your word earlier too; and you know very well what followed. Your word holds no significance!"

"But we have other things to speak," said the captain, "for one, you've made a bad mess of my ship; I haven't enough men left to sail her, and my first officer is dead. Now I have no other option but to return to the port of Glasgow. And there, you would find the redcoats to talk to you."

"Is that so?" said Alan. "Then I too will have a pretty tale for them. Fifteen sailors on one side, and a man and a boy on the other! O, man, it's pitiful!" Hoseason flushed red.

"No," continued Alan, "that will not do. You'll put me ashore as we agreed. Or, prepare for another fight."

"But, as I said, my first officer is dead," said Hoseason, "and only he was familiar with this coast that is particularly dangerous to ships."

"Safely ashore or battle; it's your choice," said Alan.

"All this will cost money," said the captain.

"Well," said Alan, "unlike you, I do not go back on my word. Thirty guineas, if you land me on the sea-side; and sixty, if you put me by the Linnhe Loch."

The captain shook his head, still frowning.

"And now, as I hear your men are a little short of brandy," said Alan, "I'll offer you an exchange: a bottle of brandy against two buckets of water."

The deal was done. The captain and Riach were happy to be able to drink again; meanwhile, Alan and I were able to wash the round-house clean.

CHAPTER 9

I Hear of the "Red Fox"

Soon, a breeze sprang up, blowing off the rain and bringing out the sun. We drove south hoping to come up to Linnhe Loch around the southern coast of the Isle of Mull.

Meanwhile, the day was very pleasant and we were sailing in a bright sunshine and with many mountainous islands upon different sides.

Alan sat smoking a pipe or two of the captain's

fine tobacco. We heard each other's stories, which was important to me as I gained knowledge of that wild Highland country on which I was so soon to land.

I began by telling Alan all my misfortunes, which he heard with great goodnature. But, when I mentioned about Mr. Campbell, the good friend of mine, Alan fired up and cried out that he hated all men of that name.

"Why," said I, upset at his talking against my well-wisher, "he is a man you should be proud to give your hand to."

"Well," he said, "he might be so. But you know very well that I am an Appin Stewart, and the Campbells have long tricked and harassed my clansmen, and seized our lands by treachery."

With that Alan banged his fist upon the table.

"The way you waste your buttons," said I, still annoyed, "I hardly think you would be a good judge of business."

"Ah!" said he, with a wry smile, "I got both,

my wastefulness as well as the buttons, from my poor father, Duncan Stewart. There was no better man or a better swordsman than him; and no one more generous. Yet, it was his generosity that left me with little or nothing after his death. That was how I came to join the English army."

"What," cried I, "were you in the English army?"

"Yes," said Alan. "This is the only black spot upon my character; but soon I crossed over to the other side - and that's some consolation for me."

"Oh," I cried, "but the punishment of desertion is death."

"Yes," said he, "if they caught me, it would mean hanging for Alan!"

"But I have the King of France's commission in my pocket, which would be some protection," he added, although doubtingly.

"But you are a condemned rebel, a deserter, and the French King's man! What brings you back into this country?" I asked him.

"I have been back every year since the last five years!" replied Alan. "France is a nice place, no doubt; but I miss my friends and country, the heather and the deer. And then I have certain things that I need to attend to. I have to pick up a few lads, new recruits to serve the King of France: but most importantly, there is the business of my chief, Ardshiel."

"I thought they called your chief Appin," said I.

"Yes, but Ardshiel is the captain of the clan," said Alan. "You see David, he, who all his life was so great a man, is now brought down to live in a French town like a poor person. Now, the tenants of Appin have to pay a rent to King George; but in their hearts they are true to their chief; and what with love and a bit of pressure, the poor folk scrape up a second rent for Ardshiel. Well, David, I'm the one that carries the money to him."

"Do the poor farmers pay two rents?" cried I.

"Yes, David, both," he told me.

"I call it noble," I cried. "I'm a supporter of King George; but still I call it noble."

"Yes" said he, "but you're a gentleman; and that's why you feel it's noble.

Now, if you were a Campbell, you would be outraged. If you were the Red Fox..."

And at that name, his teeth shut together. His face was dark with rage.

"And... who is the Red Fox?" I asked, frightened, but still curious.

"Who is he?" cried Alan, "Well, I'll tell you that. When the clans were broken at the battle of Culloden, Ardshiel had to flee like a poor deer upon the mountains – he, his lady and his children. While he still lay in the heather, and we were arranging to ship him to France, the English were striking at his rights. They stripped him of all his powers and his land. They plucked the weapons from the hands of his clansmen – men who had borne arms for thirty centuries! They took the very clothes off their backs -- so that it's now a sin to wear a tartan plaid, and a man may be put into prison if he does so.

"However, they could not destroy one thing; and that was the love the clansmen felt for their chief. These guineas – the rents are the proof of it. But then, there was a Campbell, red-headed Colin of Glenure..."

"Is that him you call the Red Fox?" said I.

"Yes, that's the man," cried Alan, fiercely. "He got a contract from King George to obtain the rent on the lands of Appin. Eventually, when he came to know how the poor folks of Appin were gathering up a second rent and sending it to Ardshiel, the black Campbell blood in him ran wild. What! A Stewart was getting all this money, and he was not able to prevent it?

"Well, David, you know what did the villain do? He got another contract from King George that enabled him to put all our farms on the market for sale. He had thought, 'I'll get other tenants who'll buy the farms of these Stewarts, and Maccolls and Macrobs' (for these all are names in my clan, David); 'and then Ardshiel will have to beg on a French roadside.'"

"Well, Alan," said I, "I am glad the man was beaten."

"Him beaten?" echoed Alan. "You know little of Campbells, and less of the Red Fox. He would never stop trying to overthrow my clansmen off their property. But if the day comes, David, no one, in all Scotland would be able to hide him from my revenge!"

"It's a known thing that Christianity forbids revenge," I cried.

"Yes," said Alan, "I can see it was a Campbell who taught you! You're good in a fight, but, man You have Whig blood in you!"

He spoke kindly enough, but there was so much anger under his contempt that I thought it was wise to change the conversation.

CHAPTER 10

The Loss of the Ship

It was already late at night when Hoseason clapped his head into the roundhouse door.

"Here," said he, "come out and see if you can navigate, my ship is in danger!"

By the sharp tones in which he spoke of his ship, it was plain to both of us he was in earnest; and we stepped on deck.

The sky was clear; but it was quite windy

and bitter cold. The Covenant tore through the seas at a great speed, pitching and straining. I had begun to wonder what worried the captain so much, when the ship rose suddenly on the top of a high swell, and Hoseason pointed to the open water: a fountain rose out of the moonlit sea, and immediately after, we heard a low sound of roaring.

"What do you call that?" asked the captain.

"The sea breaking on a reef," said Alan.

"Yes," said Hoseason, "if it was the only one."

And just as he spoke there came a second fountain farther to the south.

"There!" said Hoseason. "If I had known of these reefs, even six hundred guineas wouldn't have made me risk my ship! But you, sir, didn't you know about them?"

"I think," said Alan, "these will be what they call the Torran Rocks."

"Are there many of them?" asked the captain.

"I have heard that there are ten miles of them," said Alan.

Mr. Riach and the captain looked at each other.

"Is there a way through them?" said the captain.

"I am not sure," said Alan, "but I think it is said it is safer near the land."

"Then we have to come as near the shore of Mull as we can take her, sir," said Hoseason.

With that he gave an order to the steersman, and sent Riach to the foretop. There were only five men on deck, these being all that were fit for their work.

However, as we got nearer to the turn of the land, the reefs began to emerge here and there on our very path; and Mr. Riach sometimes cried down to us to change the course. Neither the captain nor Mr. Riach had shown well in the fighting; but I saw they were brave in their own trade.

After a while, Mr. Riach announced from the top that he saw clear water ahead.

"You have saved the ship," Hoseason told Alan.

As we were thinking that we were safe, Mr. Riach sang out, "Reef towards the windward side!"

And, almost immediately, the tide caught the ship and threw the wind out of her sails. The ship came round into the wind like a top. And the next moment, she struck the reef so forcefully, that all of us were thrown flat upon the deck.

I was on my feet in a minute, and looked out at the sea. The reef which our ship had struck was near the south west coast of Mull, and in between this coast and our ship was a little black isle called Earraid.

Meanwhile, the waves kept breaking clear over the deck, and I could hear the bottom o' the ship grounding upon the reef.

Soon, I observed Mr. Riach and the seamen

busy round the skiff and I ran over to assist them. It was no easy task, and we all worked like horses.

Meanwhile, those of the wounded who could move came out of the forecastle and began to help, while the rest that lay helpless screamed and begged to be saved.

The captain took no part. He stood still, talking to himself and groaning out aloud whenever the ship hammered on the rock. His ship was like wife and child to him; and he seemed to suffer along with her.

All the time of our working at the boat, I remember asking Alan, who was looking across at the shore, what country it was. And he answered that it was the worst possible for him, for it was a land of the Campbells.

Suddenly, the sailor who was put to keep a watch upon the seas, cried out in a shrill voice, "Hold on!"

We knew by his tone that it was something more than ordinary; and sure enough, there followed a wave so huge that it lifted up the ship and tipped her over on her beam. At this sudden tilting, I was cast clean over the bulwarks into the cold, dark sea.

I went down and drank up lots of water, then came up and got a blink of the moon, and then down again. They say a man sinks a third time for good. But I must have been made differently, for I sank below the water and rose to the surface numerous times, swallowing up water and spitting and choking.

After being tossed about for a long while, I came into calmer water, holding onto a shaft of wood I had come across. It was then that I noticed I was about a mile away from the ship. I was quite shocked, and, suddenly, started feeling cold. I began to wonder whether a man can die of cold as well as of drowning. The shores of Earraid were close in; in the moonlight I could see the dots of heather and the sparkling of the mica in the rocks.

With my little swimming experience, I did not reach the shore for a long time. Finally, after about an hour of kicking and splashing, my feet touched the sandy bottom, and I was able to wade ashore on foot.

The sea here was quite quiet. I thought I had never seen a place so empty and desolate. As I threw myself on the sandy beach, I could not tell if I was more tired or more grateful.

The Islet

With my stepping ashore Earraid, I began the unhappy part of my adventures. There was no sign of the ship, nor could I spot man on land. I was afraid to think what had befallen my shipmates. And I was worried for Alan.

By now, my belly had begun to ache with hunger. I knew that shell-fish were thought to be good to eat; and among the rocks of the isle

I found plenty of limpets. Of these, I made my whole diet, devouring them cold and raw as I found them. But, often I was seized with giddiness and retching after gulping these down my throat.

All day it rained, and there was no dry spot to be found. And when I lay down that night, between two boulders that made a kind of roof, my feet were in a swamp.

The second day, I explored the island on all sides. Not one part of it was better than another; it was all desolate and rocky. But there was a creek that cut off the isle from the mainland, but it was too wide and deep to cross. From above a hilltop, I could see a village on this mainland. During the day, I watched smoke go up from the cottage chimneys. I used to watch this smoke, when I was wet and cold, and think of the fireside and the company, till my heart burned.

On the third morning I discovered that most of the fifty pounds I had, had slipped out of a hole in my pocket. Now I was left with only two guinea-pieces and a silver shilling.

Moreover, I was in a pitiful condition. My clothes were beginning to rot; my hands had wrinkled; my throat was very sore, and I had become weak.

And yet the worst was still to come.

As soon as the sun came out, I lay down on the top of a high rock on the northwest of Earraid to dry myself. All of a sudden, I noticed a boat with a pair of fishers turning around the headland.

I shouted out, waved my hands, and prayed to them. They were near enough to hear; I could even see the color of their hair. There was no doubt that they observed me too, for they cried out in the Gaelic tongue, and laughed. But the boat moved ahead, right before my eyes!

I could not believe such wickedness, and ran along the shore, shouting and crying. I thought my heart would have burst. If a wish could kill men, those two fishers would have died then.

The next day, I observed a boat coming down

and I thought it was headed in my direction. I recognized it to be the same boat and the same two men as yesterday. But now there was a third man along with them. As soon as they had come within hearing, they drew no nearer in.

What frightened me most of all, the new man tee-hee'd with laughter as he talked and looked at me. Then, he stood up in the boat and addressed me in Gaelic for a long while, speaking and waving his hand.

I told the man I didn't understand Gaelic; and at this he became very angry. So, I began to suspect he thought he was talking in English all this while. Listening very close, I caught the word "whateffer" several times.

"Whatever," said I, to show him I had caught a word.

"Yes," he shouted back, and then he looked at the other men, as much as to say, "I told you I spoke English," and began again as hard as ever in Gaelic. This time I picked out another word,

'tide'.

Then I had a flash of hope. I remembered he was always waving his hand towards the mainland of the Ross.

"Do you mean the tide is out?" I cried.

"Yes," said he. "Tide!" And all three of them laughed again.

Immediately, I turned my back upon their boat, and leapt back the way I had come. In about half an hour, I came out upon the shores of the creek. The tide was out, and the creek was shrunk into a little trickle of water!

I dashed through the water that was not even above my knees, and landed with a shout on the main island.

A sea-bred boy would not have stayed even one day on Earraid; which was what they call a tidal islet. It could be reached during low tide twice every twenty-four hours.

If only I had sat down to think, instead of bemoaning my fate, I would have soon guessed the secret, and got free. It was no wonder the fishers had not understood me. It was rather surprising that they had at all guessed my pitiful delusion, and had taken the trouble to come back and enlighten me of my foolishness.

I had starved with cold and hunger on that island for close to one hundred hours. If it were not for the fishermen, my bones would be lying in the isle, and that, all because of my foolishness.

CHAPTER 12

The Lad with the Silver Button:
Through the Isle of Mull

I sought for the smoke I had seen so often from the island; and at last I came upon a house. On a mound in front of it, an old gentleman sat smoking his pipe in the sun.

With whatever little English he knew, he made me understand that my shipmates had got safely ashore, and had broken bread in that very house.

"Was there one," I asked, "dressed like a gentleman?"

He said that the first of them, the one that came alone, wore breeches and stockings, while the rest had sailors' trousers.

This set me smiling. I was assured that my friend Alan was safe.

Then the old gentleman clapped his hand to his brow, and cried out that I must be the lad with the silver button.

"Why, yes!" said I, in some wonder.

"Well, then," said the old gentleman, "I have a message for you, that you are to follow your friend to his own part of the country, by way of Torosay."

He took me by the hand, led me into his hut and presented me before his wife. The good woman set oat-bread before me and a cold grouse; and the old gentleman brewed me a strong punch out of their country spirit. I could hardly believe my good fortune.

The punch threw me in a deep slumber and the good people let me lie. It was nearly noon of the next day before I took the road. My spirits were quite restored.

I thought to myself: "If these are the wild Highlanders, I wish my own folk were a bit wilder."

Torosay was a grubby little town on the sea that looked across to the south coast of Scotland. I took a ferry from Torosay to Kinlochaline. Both the towns were in the country of the Mcleans, and the voyagers who crossed with me were all of that clan. The captain of the boat was called Neil Roy Macrob; and since Macrob was one of the names of Alan's clansmen, I was eager to come to private speech with Neil Roy.

At Kinlochaline I approached Neil Roy upon one side on the beach, when he was alone.

"I am seeking somebody, sir," said I; "Alan Stewart is his name."

And very foolishly, instead of showing him the button, I wanted to pass a shilling in his hand.

At this he drew back.

"I am very much offended," he said; "and this is not the way that one gentleman should behave to another at all."

I saw I had gone the wrong way, and without wasting time upon apologies, showed him the silver button I held in my hand.

"You are the lad with the silver button! Well, I have the word to see that you come safe. But if you'd pardon my plain speaking, there's a name you should never take: the name of Alan Breck; and there is another thing that you should never do, and that is to offer to buy information from a Highland gentleman."

And as Neil had no wish to prolong his dealings with me, but only to fulfill his orders and be done with it, he quickly gave me further directions.

Early in my next day's journey I overtook a little, stout man, walking slowly, sometimes reading in a book and sometimes marking the place with his finger. He was dressed plainly in something of a clerical style.

I came to know that he was a catechist named Henderland and he spoke with the broad south-country tongue which was like sweet music to my ears. Besides common country-ship, we soon found we had a more particular bond of interest. For, my good friend Mr. Campbell had translated a number of hymns and pious books into Gaelic, which were held in great esteem by Mr. Henderland.

I told him only as much of my affairs as I judged wise, and that Balachulish was the place I was traveling to, to meet a friend. I did not mention Alan.

But he had heard of Alan already.

"Alan Breck is a bold, desperate fellow, and well known to be James' right hand," said Mr. Henderland. "His life is forfeit already; he would hesitate at nothing."

"And what about Red Fox?" I asked.

"Colin Campbell?" said Mr. Henderland. "He is putting his head in a bees' hive!"

We continued talking and walking the greater part of the day, and in the afternoon we came to a small house belonging to him, standing alone by the shore of the Linnhe Loch.

Soon after we had eaten, and before we went to bed he offered me sixpence to help me on my way, out of a scanty store he kept in the turf wall of his house.

At this excess of goodness I did not know how to react. But, the kind gentleman was so earnest that I thought it more mannerly to let him have his way, and so, left him poorer than myself.

The Death of the "Red Fox"

The next day, Mr. Henderland found for me a man who had his own boat and was to cross the Linnhe Loch that afternoon into Appin, for fishing.

A short while after we had started, I noticed a little moving clump of scarlet, close along the water-side to the north. I asked my boatman what it might be. He told me that it was some of the red coats (soldiers) coming from Fort William into Appin, against the poor farmers of the country.

It was a sad sight to me. And though this was just the second time I had seen King George's troops, I was left with no good will for them.

At last we came so near the point of entrance to Loch Leven that I begged to be set on shore. My boatman would gladly have carried me on to Balachulish, (remembering his promise to Mr. Henderland). But as this would take me farther from my secret destination, I insisted, and was set on shore at last under the wood of Lettermore in Alan's country of Appin.

I sat down to eat some oat-bread of Mr. Henderland's and think upon my situation. I wondered why I was going to join myself with an outlaw and a would-be murderer like Alan, and whether I should not be acting more sensibly in tramping back to the south country, straight to my own country and people.

As I was so thinking, a sound of men and

horses came to me through the wood.

Presently, I saw four travelers come into view. The first was a heavy, redheaded gentleman, who carried his hat in his hand and fanned himself. The second, by his decent black garb and white wig, I judged to be a lawyer. The third was a servant. And as for the fourth, who was heavily armed, I knew at once to be a sheriff's officer.

When the first came alongside of me, I rose up and asked him the way to Aucharn.

The heavy man stopped and looked at me; and then, turning to the lawyer, said, "Mungo, many men would think this to be a warning! Here am I on my road to Duror, on the job you know; and here is a young lad who inquires if I am on the way to Aucharn!"

"Colin," said the other, "this is not a laughing matter."

These two had now drawn close up and were gazing at me, while the two followers had halted about a stone-cast in the rear.

"And what do you seek in Aucharn?" said Colin Roy Campbell, him they called the Red Fox. For it was he whom I had stopped.

"I am looking for James of the Glens," said I.

"James of the Glens," repeated Red Fox, broodingly; and then he turned to the lawyer, saying, "Is he gathering his people, you think?"

"Any way," said the lawyer, "we shall do better to stay where we are, and let the soldiers come here."

"If you are concerned for me," said I, "I am neither of his people nor yours, but an honest subject of King George."

"Why, very well said," replied Red Fox. "But what is this honest man doing so far from his country, and why does he come seeking the brother of Ardshiel? I have power here, I must tell you, and have twelve files of soldiers at my back."

"I have heard," said I, a little annoyed, "that you were a tough man to drive."

He still kept looking at me, as if in doubt.

"Well," said he, at last, "if you had asked me the way to the door of James Stewart on any other day but this, I would have set you on the right way. But, today…"

While he was speaking, a single shot rang out and hit Red Fox. He fell upon the road.

"O, I am dead!" he cried, several times over.

The lawyer had caught him up and held him

in his arms, the servant standing over and clasping his hands. And now the wounded man looked from one to another with scared eyes.

"Take care of yourselves," he said. "I am dead."

With that he gave a great sigh, his head rolled on his shoulder, and he passed away.

The lawyer never said a word, but his face was as white as the dead man's; the servant broke out into a great noise of crying and weeping, like a child; and I, on my side, stood staring at them in a kind of horror. The sheriff's officer had run back at the first sound of the shot, to hasten the coming of the soldiers.

At last the lawyer laid down the dead man upon the road, and got to his own feet with a kind of stagger.

I believe it was his movement that brought me to my senses; for he had no sooner done so than I began to scramble up the hill, crying out "The murderer!

The murderer!"

When I got to the top of the first steepness, and could see some part of the open mountain, the murderer was still moving away at no great distance. He was a big man, in a black coat, with metal buttons, and carried a long shot-gun.

"Here!" I cried. "I see him!"

I continued to chase him until the murderer disappeared.

All this time I had been running; I had got a good way up, when a voice called upon me to stand still. When I halted and looked back, I saw all the open part of the hill below me. The lawyer and the sheriff's officer were standing just above the road, waving me to come back.

"Why should I come back?" I cried.

"Ten pounds if you take that lad!" cried the lawyer. "He's an accomplice. He was posted here to hold us in talk."

At that word my heart came in my mouth. I was all amazed and helpless.

The soldiers began to spread, some of them to run; and still I stood.

"Duck in here among the trees," said a voice close by.

I obeyed and as I did so, I heard the guns firing. Just inside the shelter of the trees I found Alan standing, with a fishing-rod.

"Come!" he cried, and set off running and I followed him. I remember seeing with wonder, that Alan every now and then would straighten himself to his full height and look back; and every time he did so, there came a great far-away crying of the soldiers.

Quarter of an hour later, Alan stopped, clapped down flat in the heather, and turned to me.

"Now," said he, "it's earnest. Do as I do, for your life."

And at the same speed, we traced back again across the mountain-side by the same way that we had come, till, at last, Alan threw himself down in the upper wood of Lettermore, where I had found him at the first. He lay, with his face in the bracken, panting like a dog.

My own sides ached so, and my tongue so hung out of my mouth with heat and dryness that I lay beside him like one dead.

CHAPTER 14

I Talk with Alan in the Wood of Lettermore

A lan was the first to come round.

"Well," said he, "that was a hot chase, David."

I said nothing. I had seen the man Alan hated murdered, and here was Alan prowling in the trees and running from the troops; and whether his was the hand that fired or the head that ordered it, mattered little.

My only friend in that wild country was a cold-blooded murderer.

"Are you still tired?" he asked again.

"No," said I, "no, I am not tired now, and I can speak. We must part. I liked you very well, Alan, but your ways are not mine."

"I will hardly part from you, David, without some kind of reason for the same," said Alan.

"Alan," said I, "what is the sense of this? You know very well that a Campbellman lies in his blood upon the road."

"I will tell you first of all that if I were going to kill a gentleman, it would not be in my own country, to bring trouble upon my clan. And I would not go murdering people with a long fishing-rod upon my back," said he.

"Well," I agreed, "that's true!"

"And now," continued Alan, taking out his dirk and laying his hand upon it in a certain manner, "I swear upon the Holy Iron I had neither art nor part, act nor thought in it."

"I thank God for that!" I cried, and offered him my hand.

He did not appear to see it.

"And here is a great deal of work about a Campbell!" said he. "They are not so scarce, that I know!"

"At least," said I, "you can't blame me for thinking that you were involved, for you know very well what you told me on the ship."

"And do you know who did it?" I added. "Do you know that man in the black coat?"

"I have no clear mind about his coat," said Alan cunningly, "but it sticks in my head that it was blue."

"Blue or black, did you know him?" said I.

"It's strange, but I was tying my shoes when he ran past me," said Alan.

"Can you swear that you don't know him, Alan?" I cried.

"Not yet," he replied; "but I've a grand memory for forgetting, David."

"And yet there was one thing I saw clearly," said I; "that you exposed yourself to the soldiers to protect me."

"So would any gentleman," said Alan. "You were innocent of that matter."

I knew Alan was trying to protect the murderer, but he had also endangered his life to protect me.

Mr. Henderland's words came back to me: that we ourselves might take a lesson by these wild Highlanders. Well, here I had taken mine. Alan's morals were all tail-first; but he was ready to give his life for them, such as they were.

Alan said we had not much time to waste, but must both flee that country: he, because he was a deserter, and the whole of Appin would now be searched like a chamber; and I, because I was certainly involved in the murder.

"O!" I said, willing to give him a little lesson, "I have no fear of the justice of my country."

"As if this was your country!" said he. "O

as if you would be tried here, in a country of Stewarts!"

I was sceptical, but was finally persuaded that it was safer to follow Alan than trust the Campbell's justice system.

So, we rested for an hour, as the soldiers searched for us far off.

Night fell as we were walking. At about half-past ten, we came to the top of a hill, and saw lights below us. It seemed a house door stood open and let out a beam of fire and candle-light; and all round the house five or six persons were moving hurriedly about, each carrying a torch.

Then, Alan whistled three times. It was strange to see how, at the first sound of it, all the moving torches came to a stand, as if the bearers were frightened.

Then, at the third whistle, the bustle began again as before. So, we came down the hill, and were met at the yard gate by a tall, handsome man who cried out to Alan in the Gaelic.

"James Stewart," said Alan, "I will ask you to speak in Scotch, for here is a young gentleman with me who knows not the other."

"This is him," Alan added, putting his arm through mine, "a young gentleman of the Lowlands, but I am thinking it will be the better if we do not call him by his name."

James turned to me for a moment, and greeted me courteously; then, he turned to Alan.

"This has been a dreadful accident," he cried. "It will bring trouble on the country."

"Hoots!" said Alan, "you must take the sour with the sweet. After all, Colin Roy is dead!"

"But, I wish he was alive again!" said James. "The accident fell out in Appin – mind that, Alan and it's Appin that would have to pay. And I am a family man."

James was continually turning about from his talk with Alan, to cry out orders to the others James gave us each a sword and pistols; with these, and some ammunition, a bag of oatmeal an iron pan, and a bottle of right French brandy, we were ready for the heather.

Money, indeed, was lacking. I had about two guineas left; Alan's belt had been despatched by another hand. And as for James, he had brought himself so low with journeys to Edinburgh and legal expenses on behalf of the tenants, that he could only scrape together a few shillings.

"It's not enough," said Alan.

"I need some time to gather more money. Meanwhile, you must find a safe place somewhere near by," said James, "and get word sent to me and I will send over some cash to you."

I could see that Alan was quite uneasy about the plan.

When it was time for us to leave, Mrs. Stewart leaped out of her chair, came running over to us, and wept first upon my neck and then on Alan's, blessing God for our goodness to her family.

Then, we said farewell, and set out.

CHAPTER 15

The Flight in the Heather: The Rocks

Sometimes we walked, sometimes we ran; and as it drew on to morning, we walked ever less and ran all the more.

Though, upon its face, that country appeared to be a desert, yet there were huts and houses of the people, of which we must have passed more than twenty, hidden in quiet places of the hills.

The day began to break while we were sti

far from any shelter. We found ourselves in a remarkable valley strewn with rocks; a foaming river ran by it. Wild mountains stood around it; there grew neither grass nor trees. I could see Alan knit his brow.

"This is no fit place for you and me," he said. "This is a place they're bound to watch."

And with that he ran harder than ever down to the water-side, in a part where the river was split in two among three rocks. It went through with a horrid thundering that made my belly quake. Alan looked neither to the right nor to the left, but jumped clean upon the middle rock and fell there on his hands and knees to check himself, for that rock was small and he might have pitched over on the far side. I had scarce time to measure the distance or to understand the peril before I had followed him, and he had caught and topped me.

So there we stood, side by side upon a small rock slippery with spray, a far broader leap in front of us, and the river dinning upon all sides. When I saw where I was, there came upon me a deadly sickness of fear, and I put my hand over my eyes. The next minute Alan had set the brandy bottle to my lips, and forced me to drink about a gill, which sent the blood into my head again.

Then, he shouted into my ears, "Hang or drown!" and turning his back upon me, leaped over the farther branch of the stream, and landed safe.

I was now alone upon the rock; the brandy was singing in my ears; I had just wit enough to see that if I did not leap at once, I should never leap at all. I bent low on my knees and flung myself forth. It was my hands that reached the full length, and these slipped, caught again, slipped again; and I was sliding back into the water, when Alan seized me, and with a great strain, dragged me to safety.

Without saying a word, Alan set off running again for his life, and I stumbled after him. I wa sick and bruised, and partly drunken; and at last we paused under a great rock that stood there among a number of others.

It was actually two rocks leaning together at the top, both some twenty feet high. Both of us scrambled up with quite a lot of difficulty.

Then I saw why we had come there; for the two rocks, being both somewhat hollow on the top and sloping one to the other, made a kind of cavern, where as many as three or four men might have lain hidden.

Alan clapped flat down. Then, keeping only one eye above the edge of our place of shelter, scouted all round the area.

Then, at last Alan smiled.

"Yes, now we have a chance;" and then looking at me with some amusement, "You're not very good at the jumping," said he.

Then, he added at once, "Hoots! Small blame to you! To be afraid of a thing and yet to do it, is what makes the bravest kind of a man. Get some sleep, and I'll watch," said Alan.

Accordingly, I lay down to sleep.

In the morning when I was roughly awakened, I found Alan's hand pressed upon my mouth.

"Wheesht!" he whispered. "You were snoring."

"Well," said I, surprised at his anxious face, "and why not?"

He peeped over the edge of the rock, and signed to me to do the like.

It was now high day, cloudless, and very hot. The valley was as clear as in a picture. About half a mile up the water was a camp of red-coats; and on the top of a rock about as high as ours, there stood a sentry. All the way down along the river-side were posted other sentries. I took but one look at them, and ducked again into my place.

"You see," said Alan, "this was what I was afraid of, Davie: that they would watch the burn-side. They began to come in about two hours ago. If they get up the sides of the hill, they could easily

spy us with a glass. The posts are less down the water; and, when it is night, we'll try our hand at getting by them."

"And what are we to do till night?" I asked.

"Lie here," he replied.

The sun beat upon us cruelly; the rock grew so heated, a man could scarce endure its touch. We took turns to lie on the naked rock. All the while we had no water but only raw brandy for a drink.

And at last, the sun got a little into the west, and there came a patch of shade on the east side of our rock - which was the side sheltered from the soldiers.

"It's better to die this way, than being scorched to death," said Alan, and dropped on the ground on the shadowy side. I followed him. Here, we lay for an hour, aching from head to foot and lying quite exposed to the eye of any soldier who should have strolled that way. However, none came.

Presently, we began to get a little strength; and as the soldiers were now lying closer along the river-side, Alan proposed that we should try a start. So we got ourselves at once in marching order, and began to slip from rock to rock, one after the other. The soldiers, having searched this side of the valley, stood dozing at their posts or only kept a look-out along the banks of the river.

So, we drew steadily away from their

neighborhood.

By sundown we had made some distance. Now we came on something that put all fears out of season; and that was a deep rushing stream, that tore down in that part, to join the glen river.

We cast ourselves on the ground, and plunged our heads and shoulders in the water.

And at last, being refreshed, we got out the meal-bag, mixed cold water with oatmeal, and ate the simple meal. It made a good enough dish for two hungry men. At night, we set forth again.

CHAPTER 16

The Flight in the Heather:
The Heugh of Corrynakiegh

It was still dark when we reached a cleft, called the Heugh of Corrynakiegh, in the head of a great mountain. A lake ran through its center; and on one side there was a shallow cave in a rock surrounded by a wood of pines.

The lake was full of trout, and the wood, of doves and cuckoos. From the mouth of the cleft we could look down upon a part of Mamore, and on the water body that divided that country from Appin. And this from so great a height, that it was both wonderful and enjoyable to sit and behold them.

It was on the whole a pleasant place, and the five days we lived here, went happily.

We slept in the cave, making our bed of heather bushes. We could make a small fire in the cave without the fear of detection, so that we could warm ourselves when the clouds set in, and cook hot porridge, and grill the little trout that we caught in the lake.

"Now we must get word sent to James, and he must find the money for us," Alan said to me on our first morning.

Then he fell in a thoughtful silence, looking in the embers of the fire. Presently, he got a piece of wood, cut it in two, and fastened them in a cross. Next, he blackened the four ends with the coals. Then he looked at me a little shyly.

"Could you lend me my button?" he asked. "It seems a strange thing to ask a gift again, but I don't want to cut another."

He strung the button on a strip of his greatcoat which he had used to bind the cross. Then he tied a little sprig of birch and one of fir to the cross, and then looked upon his work with satisfaction.

"Now," said he, "there is a little clachan (what is called a hamlet) not very far from Corrynakiegh, and it has the name of Koalisnacoan. Many friends of mine live there, whom I could trust with my life. So when it comes dark again, I will steal down into that clachan, and set this cross in the window of John Breck, a good friend of mine."

"And if he finds it, what is he to think?" I asked.

"Well," Alan said, "I can only hope that he will understand my message, which is this: this cross is the signal of gathering in our clans; but John will know well enough the clan is not to gather, for there is no note attached telling him where to go. So, he will understand that there is something else. Then he will see my button, and that was my father's, Duncan Stewart's. And then he will say to himself, that the son of Duncan is in the heather, and needs my help."

"Well," said I, "it may be. But even if he understands your message, how will he know where to find you?"

"But then John Breck will see the sprig of birch and the sprig of pine;" said Alan, "and he will say to himself, Alan will be lying in a wood which has both pines and birches. Then he will come and give us a look up in Corrynakiegh. And if he does not figure it out, David, then he isn't worth the salt in his porridge."

So, that night Alan carried down his fiery cross and set it in John Breck's window. The next day we lay in the borders of the wood and kept a close lookout. About noon we saw a man straggling up the open side of the mountain in the sun, and looking round him as he came. No sooner had Alan seen him than he whistled; the man turned and, guided by the sound of whistling, reached to the spot where we lay.

He was a ragged, wild, bearded man, of about forty.

However, he refused to take a message for James, unless it was in the form of a letter. I thought Alan would be puzzled at that, for we lacked the means of writing. But Alan was a man of more resources; he searched the wood until he found the quill of a dove, which he shaped into a pen; he made himself a kind of ink with gunpowder from his pistol and water from the running stream; and, tearing a corner from his French military commission, he sat down and wrote:

DEAR KINSMAN,

Please send the money by the bearer to the place he knows of.

Your affectionate cousin,

A. S.

This he entrusted to John, who promised to be back as quickly as possible.

About five in the evening of the third day, we heard a whistling in the wood, which Alan answered. Presently John came up the water-side, looking for us. He gave us the news of the country; that it was swarming with red-coats. James and some of his servants were already clapped in prison at Fort William, under strong suspicion of complicity in the murder. It was rumored all around that Alan Breck had fired the shot; and there was a reward of a hundred pounds issued for both him and me.

The little note John had brought us from Mrs. Stewart was of a miserable sadness. In it she besought Alan not to let himself be captured. The money she had sent was all that she could beg or borrow, and she prayed heaven we could manage with it.

"It's little enough," said Alan, putting the money in his pocket, "but it'll do my business. And now, John Breck, if you will hand me over my button, we will be heading for the road."

And so, the button was returned to us.

CHAPTER 17

The Flight in the Heather: The Moor

Early in the morning we were at the end of a range of mountains. In front of us there lay a piece of low, broken, desert land. The sun was not long up, and shone straight in our eyes.

We sat down, and made ourselves some porridge.

"David," said Alan, "this is how we stand: behind us is Appin; going there could mean death for us. To the south is the land of the Campbells. To the north; well, nothing can be gained by going north; neither for you, that wants to get to Queensferry, nor for me, that wants to get to France. Well, then, we can strike east," suggested Alan.

"East be it!" I said, but at the same time I was thinking: 'If you would only take one point of the compass and let me take any other, it would be the best for both of us.'

"Well, then, east we go," said Alan. "But once there, David, it's a big risk. There is no place in that bald, bare and flat land, where a person would be able to hide himself. If the red-coats come over a hill, they can spy us miles away; and soon they would hunt us down."

"Alan," said I, "it's all a risk; but I give you my word that I will keep going ahead until we drop."

Alan was delighted.

"There are times," said he, "when you are altogether too much of a King George's man for my liking; but there are others when your courage sparks. And it's then, David, that I love you like a brother."

The mist died away and showed us the country lying as waste as the sea. Much of it was red with heather; much of the rest, broken up with swamps and muddy pools.

We went down into the waste and started on our toilsome travel.

All round there were the tops of mountains from where we might be spotted any moment; so it was necessary to keep in the hollow parts of the moor.

Toiling and resting we moved ahead, and at about noon lay down in a thick bush of heather to sleep.

Alan took the first watch. It seemed to me I had scarcely closed my eyes before Alan shook me awake to take the second watch.

We had no clock to go by; and thus Alan stuck a sprig of heath in the ground, so that as soon as

the shadow of the bush should fall so far to the east, I might know it was time to rouse him.

But I was by this time so weary that I could have slept twelve hours at a stretch. I had the taste of sleep in my throat and my joints slept even when my mind was waking. Every now and then I would give a little shake, and discover that I had been dozing all the while.

The last time I woke up, I looked at the sprig

of heath, and almost cried aloud: for I saw I had betrayed my trust. And then, when I turned my head and looked out around me on the moor, my heart almost stopped beating. A body of horse soldiers had come down during my sleep, and were drawing near to us from the south-east.

When I awakened Alan, he glanced first at the soldiers, then at the mark and the position of the sun, and knitted his brows with a sudden, quick look.

"What are we to do now?" I asked.

"We'll have to play at being the rabbits," said he. "Do you see that mountain?" pointing to one on the north-eastern sky.

"Yes," said I.

"Its name is Ben Alder," said Alan, "it is a wild, desert mountain full of hills and hollows, and if we can reach it before morning, we might be safe."

"But, Alan," cried I, "that will take us across the path of the soldiers!"

"I know that," said he; "but we can't go back

now. So now, David, be fast!"

With that he began to run forward on his hands and knees with an incredible speed, and I followed as best as I could. Alan kept winding in and out in the lower parts of the moorland where we were the best concealed. Some of these had been burned with fire; and there rose in our faces a blinding, choking dust as fine as smoke. The water was long out; and this posture of running on the hands and knees caused us tremendous weakness and weariness, and our joints groaned and ached under our weight.

Now and then, we halted a little where there was a big bush of heather, and putting aside the leaves, looked back at the dragoons. The soldiers had not spotted us, for they held straight on; a half-troop, I think, covering about two miles of ground, and beating the heather mighty thoroughly as they went. They were ensuring that no one was hiding there. Now and then a rustle rose out of the heather, and we lay as still as the dead, and were afraid to even breathe.

The aching of my body, the soreness of my hands, and the continual smoke of dust and ashes had soon grown to be so unbearable that I would gladly have given up. Nothing but the fear of Alan lent me enough of a false kind of courage to continue. As for Alan, I was driven to wonder at the man's power of endurance.

At length, in the first gloaming of the night, we heard a trumpet sound, and looking back from among the heather, saw the troop beginning to collect. A little after, they had built a fire and camped for the night, in about the middle of the waste.

At this I begged Alan that we might now lie down and sleep.

"There shall be no sleep this night!" said Alan.

"Alan," I said, "I don't have the strength to go on any longer."

"Very well, then," said Alan. "I'll carry you."

The sight of so much resolution shamed me.. "Lead away!" said I. "I'll follow."

He gave me one look as much as to say, "Well done, David!" and off he set again at his top speed.

Day began to come in, after years and years, as I thought. And by that time we were past the greatest danger, and could walk upon our feet like men, instead of crawling like animals.

But, what a pair we must have made, bending double like old grandfathers, stumbling like babies, and as white as dead folk. Never a word passed between us; each set his mouth and kept his eyes in front of him, and lifted up his foot and set it down again, like people lifting weights at a country play.

Alan must have been as stupid with weariness as myself, and looked as little where we were going, or we should not have walked into an ambush like blind men.

It fell in this way:

We were going down a heathery slope, Alan leading and I following a pace or two behind. Suddenly, the heather gave a rustle, four men leaped out, and the next moment we were lying on our backs, each with a dirk at his throat.

I heard Alan and another whispering in the Gaelic.

Then the dirks were put up, our weapons were taken away, and we were set face to face, sitting in the heather.

"They are Cluny's men," said Alan. "We could not have been captured better. We're just to bide here with these, which are his out-sentries, till they can get word to the chief of my arrival."

Alan told me that Cluny Macpherson was the chief of the clan Vourich, and had been one of the leaders of the great rebellion, six years before. There was a price on Cluny's head, just like us.

Soon, the messenger returned with the news that Cluny had called for us. His men led us to his cave. As I was feverish, the men had to carry me.

CHAPTER 18

Cluny's Cage

We came at last to the foot of a steep wood, which scrambled up a craggy hillside. Quite at the top, and just before the rocky face of the cliff sprang above the foliage, we found that strange house which was known in the country as "Cluny's Cage."

Cluny's Cage was large enough to shelter six persons with some comfort. A projection of the cliff had been cunningly employed to be the fireplace; and the smoke rising against the face of the rock, readily escaped notice from below.

When we came to the door he was seated by his rock chimney, watching a gillie (a servant) doing some cookery. Cluny had the manners of a king, and it was quite a sight to see him rise out of his place to welcome us.

"Come, Mr. Stewart!" said he, "and bring in your friend whose name I do not know."

"And how are you, Cluny?" said Alan. "I hope you do well, sir. And I am proud to see you, and to present to you my friend the Laird of Shaws, Mr. David Balfour."

"Step in by, the both of you, gentlemen," said Cluny. "I welcome you to my house, which is a queer, rude place for certain, but one where I have entertained a royal personage. We'll take a dram for luck, and then we'll dine and take a hand at the cards as gentlemen should. And so, here's a toast to you: The Restoration!"

Thereupon, we all drank. I am sure I wished no ill to King George; and if he had been there himself in proper person, it's like he would have done as I did.

It was certainly a strange place, and we had a strange host. In his long hiding, Cluny had grown to have all manners and precise habits like those of an old maid. He had a particular place where no one else must sit; the Cage was arranged in a particular way; cookery was one of his chief fancies, and even while he was greeting us in, he kept an eye on the roasting meat.

The first thing in the morning, a barber came and shaved him, and gave him the news of the country, of which he was immoderately greedy.

On that first day, after finishing the meal, Cluny took out an old deck of cards.

At first I thought of making an excuse of being exhausted, but then I decided that I should speak my mind. I told Cluny that I did not think it was right to play cards and so, I would rather not.

The chief let out a gasp. However, Alan tried to explain that though I was a Whig, I was a good boy and should be allowed to rest. I confirmed my exhaustion and explained that I was following my father's wishes.

So, Cluny agreed, and I was shown to a bed of heather.

What with the brandy and the meat, a strange heaviness had come over me; and I had scarcely lain down upon the bed before I fell into a kind of trance, in which I continued almost the whole time of our stay in the Cage.

The barber-gillie, who was a doctor too, was called in to prescribe for me; but as he spoke in the Gaelic, I understood not a word of his opinion, and was too sick even to ask for a translation.

I knew well enough I was ill, and that was all I cared about. I paid little heed while I lay in this poor pass. But Alan and Cluny were most of the time at the cards.

The second day, about noon I was wakened as usual for my meal, and as usual refused to eat. Cluny sat at the table, biting the pack of cards. Alan had stooped over the bed, and had his face close to my eyes.

He asked me for a loan of my money.

"What for?" said I.

"Hut, David!" said Alan, "you cannot give me a loan?"

I would, though, if I had had my senses! But I

handed him my money.

On the morning of the third day, I awoke with a great relief of spirits, but very weak. I had breakfast, and then sat down outside the Cage in the cool, mild air.

When I returned, Cluny and Alan had laid the cards aside, and were talking to a gillie. I saw cards on the table, but no gold; only a heap of little written papers, and these all on Cluny's side. Alan, besides, had an odd look, like a man not very well content.

I began to have a strong misgiving.

"I do not know if I am as well as I should be," said I, looking at Alan; "but the little money we have has a long way to carry us."

Alan took his under-lip into his mouth, and looked upon the ground.

"David," he said at last, "I've lost it; there's the bare truth. Your money too," continued Alan, with a groan; "you shouldn't have given it to me. I'm silly and mad when I get to the cards."

"Hoot-toot!" said Cluny. "It's all nonsense. Of course you'll have your money back again. It would be an odd thing for me to keep it!" he cried.

Alan said nothing.

"Will you step to the door with me, sir?" said I.

Cluny followed me readily enough, but he looked flustered and put out.

"And now, sir," I said, "I must first acknowledge your generosity."

"Nonsense!" cried Cluny. "Where's the generosity? This is just a most unfortunate affair; but what would you have me do -- boxed up in this cage of mine -- but just sit with my friends at the cards when I can get them? And if they lose, of course, it's not to be supposed..."

And here he came to a pause.

"Yes," said I, "if they lose, you give them back their money; and if they win, they carry away yours in their pouches! I have said before that I

146

grant your generosity; but to me, sir, it's a very painful thing to be placed in this position."

There was a little silence, in which Cluny seemed always as if he was about to speak, but said nothing.

"I ask your advice now. Advise me as you would your son. My friend fairly lost his money; can I accept it back again? Would that be the right part for me to play? Whatever I do, you can see for yourself it must be hard upon a man of any pride."

Cluny looked me with a warlike eye, and I saw the challenge at his lips.

"Mr. Balfour," said he, "I think you are too nice, but for all that you have the spirit of a very pretty gentleman. Upon my honest word, you may take this money."

CHAPTER 19

The Flight in the Heather: The Quarrel

Alan and I were put across Loch Errocht at night, and went to another hidingplace near the head of Loch Rannoch, where we were led by one of the gillies from the Cage.

For a long time, we said nothing, marching alongside or one behind the other.

The thought of a separation had always run strongly in my mind. Moreover, Alan had behaved like a child, and what was worse, a treacherous child. Wheedling my money from me while I lay half-conscious was scarcely better than theft.

At last, upon the other side of Loch Errocht, going over a smooth, rushy place, Alan could bear it no longer and came close to me.

"David," he said, "this is no way for two friends to take a small accident. I have to say that I'm sorry. And now if you have anything, you'd better say it."

"O," I said, "I have nothing."

Alan seemed disconcerted. And at this I obtained a mean pleasure.

"No," said he, with a rather trembling voice, "but when I say I was to blame?"

"Why, of course you were to blame," said I, coolly; "and you will admit the fact that I have never reproached you."

At this, Alan said nothing.

We fell back into our former silence; and came to our journey's end, and supped, and lay down to sleep, without another word.

When we reached the Loch, Alan and the gillie disagreed on their course of action. The gillie finally won and took us into Campbell territory. We set forth and for the best part of three nights traveled on eerie mountains and among the well-heads of wild rivers, often buried in mist, almost continually rained upon. By day, we lay and slept in the drenching heather; by night, we constantly climbed upon break-neck hills.

We often wandered; we were often so caught up in fog that we had to lie quiet till it lightened. Our only food was porridge and a portion of cold meat that we had carried from the Cage.

This was a dreadful time; it was horribly cold all the time and my teeth chattered in my head. I had a painful stitch in my side, which never left me. During all these horrid wanderings, we almost did not talk to each other. The truth is that I was sickening for my grave. But besides that I was of an unforgiving disposition from my birth:

slow to take offence, slower to forget it. For the best part of two days Alan was untiringly kind. He was silent, indeed, but always ready to help.

The peep of the third day found us upon a very open hill, so that we could not rest down to eat and sleep. Before we had reached a place of shelter, the grey had come pretty clear, for though it still rained, the clouds ran higher. Alan, looking in my face, showed some marks of concern.

"You had better let me take your pack," said he, for perhaps the ninth time since we had parted from the scout beside Loch Rannoch.

"I do very well, I thank you," said I, as cold as ice.

Alan flushed darkly.

"I'll not offer it again," he said. "I'm not a patient man, David."

"I never said you were," said I.

Alan made no answer at the time, but his conduct answered for him. Henceforth, it is to be thought, he quite forgave himself for the affair

at Cluny's; cocking his hat again and walking gaily, he looked at me upon one side with a provoking smile.

The third night we were to pass through Balquhidder. It came clear and cold, with a touch in the air like frost, and a northerly wind that blew the clouds away. I was dead weary and full of pains. In this poor state I had to bear from my companion something in the nature of a persecution.

At last I began to feel that I could trail myself no farther.

And with that, there came on me all at once the wish to have it out with Alan, let my anger blaze, and be done with my life in a more sudden manner. He had just called me "Whig."

I stopped.

"Mr. Stewart," said I, "you should know your manners. I thought when people had a difference of opinion, gentlemen always showed their differences in a civil way."

Alan had stopped opposite to me. He listened, smiling evilly, as I could see by the starlight. And when I had finished talking, he began to whistle a Jacobite air.

"Why do you take that air, Mr. Stewart?" said I. "Is that to remind me you have been beaten on both sides?"

The air stopped on Alan's lips.

"David!" said he.

"But it's time these manners ceased," I

153

continued; "and I mean you shall henceforth speak civilly of my King and my good friends, the Campbells."

"Do you know that you insult me?" said Alan.

"I am sorry for that," said I, "for I am not done. You have been chased in the field by the grown men of my party; it seems a poor kind of pleasure to out-face a boy. Both the Campbells and the Whigs have beaten you; you have run before them like a hare. It would be proper for you to speak of them as of your betters."

Alan stood quite still, the tails of his great-coat clapping behind him in the wind.

"This is a pity," he said, at last. "There are things said that cannot be passed over."

"I never asked you to," said I. "I am as ready as yourself."

"Ready?" said he.

"Ready," I repeated. "Then, come on!"

And drawing my sword, I fell on guard as Alan

himself had taught me.

"David!" he cried. "Are you silly? I cannot draw upon you, David. It's fair murder."

"That was your look-out when you insulted me," said I.

"It's the truth!" cried Alan. "It's the bare truth," he said, and drew his sword.

But before I could touch his blade with mine, he had thrown his sword away and it fell to the ground.

"No, no …I cannot, I cannot," he kept saying.

At this, the last of my anger oozed all out of me; and I found myself only sick, and sorry. I remembered all of Alan's past kindness and courage, and how he had always helped me.

Then I recalled my own insults, and saw that I had lost for ever that good friend. The sickness I had been feeling seemed to redouble, and the pang in my side was like a sword for sharpness. I thought I must have swooned where I stood.

This it was that gave me an idea. No apology could blot out what I had said; but where an apology was useless, a mere cry for help might bring Alan back to my side. I put my pride away from me.

"Alan!" I said; "if you cannot help me, I must just die here."

He started up, and looked at me.

"It's true," said I. "Take me into a house - I'll die there easier."

"Can you walk?" asked Alan.

"No," said I, "not without help. If I die, you'll forgive me, Alan? In my heart, I liked you fine - even when I was the angriest."

"Shhh, shh!" cried Alan. "Don't say that! David man, you can …" He shut his mouth upon a sob.

"Let me get my arm about you," he continued; "that's the way! Now lean upon me hard. We're in Balwhidder; there should be no lack of houses – friends' houses here."

"Yes," said I, "I can walk this way;" and I pressed his arm with my hand. Again he came near sobbing.

"Davie," said he, "I'm not a right man at all. I have neither sense nor kindness; I could not remember you were just a boy, I couldn't see you were dying on your feet. Davie, you'll have to try and forgive me."

At the door of the first house we came to, Alan knocked, which was of no very safe enterprise in that part of the Highlands.

However, luck was with us; for, it was a household of Maclarens that we found, where Alan was not only welcome for his name's sake, but known by reputation.

Here, I was attended to without delay, and a doctor fetched.

CHAPTER 20

End of the Flight: We Pass the Forth

The month was not yet out, when I was pronounced well. We had to think of hurrying now. We were left with so little money that if we did not soon meet Mr. Rankeillor, or if on meeting him he failed to help me, we would surely starve.

Alan and I began preparing for our journey.

In Alan's view, the hunt must have now greatly

slackened; and so we would be able to cross the Stirling Bridge, which was the main pass over that river, quite easily.

Thus, one night we set out toward Stirling Bridge. We came to the edge of the hills and saw Stirling underfoot, as flat as a pancake, with the town and castle on a hill in the midst of it, and the moon shining on the Links of Forth.

I pressed for crossing the bridge right away, but Alan was wary. There seemed to be no guard but Alan advised that we lay low.

So, we waited until it grew darker.

Late at night we watched an old woman go across the bridge. She went unbothered for a while, until, suddenly, a guard who had most probably just awakened, stopped her.

We knew we had no chance to get across with the guard awake. Alan crawled further away from the bridge and I was forced to follow. I was filled with great disappointment.

"Well?" said I.

"Well," said Alan, "we have to go east!"

"And why go east?" I asked.

"O, just upon the chance!" said he. "If we cannot pass the river, we'll have to see what we can do at the sea."

"Well," said I, "but a river can be swum."

"By them that have the skill of it," returned he; "but neither of us knows how to swim well enough."

"I'm not up to you in talking back, Alan," said I, "but I can see we're making bad worse. If it's hard to pass a river, it must be worse to pass a sea."

"But there's such a thing as a boat," said Alan.

"Yes, and such a thing as money," said I. "But we have neither."

"David," said Alan, "I cannot beg, borrow, nor yet steal a boat; I'll make one!"

"Then," said I, "we will have a boat on the wrong side of the river - somebody must have brought it -- the country-side will all be in a buzz…"

"Man!" cried Alan, "If I make a boat, I'll make a person to take it back again!"

And indeed, Alan did so!

At about ten in the morning, we came to the little clachan of Limekilns. This is a place that sits near in by the water-side, and looks across the Hope to the town of Queensferry. Smoke went up from both of these, and from other villages and farms upon all hands.

In Limekilns we entered a small change-house and bought some bread and cheese from a good-looking girl. This we carried with us to a nearby wood to eat at leisure.

Sitting there, Alan devised a plan. He planned to make the pretty girl at the inn feel sorry for me so that she would help us get a boat. I did not want to trick the girl, but finally I agreed.

Accordingly, Alan went to her and told her how ill I was and how much we needed to cross the river because we were in trouble. The girl felt very sorry for me but was not convinced to help, until Alan told her how I wanted to see Mr. Rankeillor. I also mentioned that I was loyal to King George.

With these references, the girl decided we were good people, and agreed to help. She told us to hide down by the water in the woods.

We remained there the whole day, and finally, late at night, we noticed a boat coming towards us, rowed by the girl herself.

She had trusted no one else, but waited until her father was asleep and took us across the river.

She would accept no thanks, but dropped us off on the opposite shore and paddled quickly back.

CHAPTER 21

I Come to Mr. Rankeillor

The next day, it was agreed that as soon as it was dark, Alan should lie in the fields by the roadside near to Newhalls, and stir not, until he heard me whistling. Meanwhile, I proceeded to search for Mr. Rankeillor.

I was in the long street of Queensferry before the sun was up. It was a fairly built town, with good stone houses. Nevertheless, I found the town-hall not as fine as that of Peebles or the street so elegant.

But altogether, it made me ashamed for my dirty and tattered appearance.

I also realized that I had no proof of my identity and wondered whether Mr. Rankeillor would even allow me to speak.

I wandered in front of a large house with a dog lying in front of it. I envied the dumb brute who was lying lazily and carefree.

Meanwhile, a man came out of the house and walked towards me. I asked him for directions to Mr. Rankeillor.

"Why," said he, "that is his house that I have just come out of; and I am that very man."

I immediately asked for an interview.

"I do not know your name," said he, "nor yet your face."

"My name is David Balfour," said I.

"David Balfour?" he repeated, in rather a high tone, like one surprised. "And where have you come from, Mr. David Balfour?" he asked.

"I have come from a great many strange places, sir," said I; "but I think it would be as well to tell you where and how in a more private manner."

He seemed to muse awhile, holding his lip in his hand, and looking now at me and now upon the ramp of the street.

"Yes," he said, "that will be the best, no doubt."

And he led me back with him into his house and brought me into a little dusty chamber. Here he sat down, and bade me be seated.

"And now," he said; "if you have any business, pray be brief and come swiftly to the point. Nec gemino bellum Trojanum orditur ab ovo --do you understand that?" said he, with a keen look.

"I will even do as Horace says, sir," I answered, "and carry you in medias res."

He nodded as if he was well pleased, and indeed his scrap of Latin had been set to test me. For all that, and though I was somewhat encouraged, the blood came in my face when I added, "I have reason to believe myself some rights on the estate of Shaws."

"Well, Mr. Balfour," said he, "you must continue. Where were you born?"

"In Essendean, sir," said I, "the year 1733, the 12th of March."

He seemed to follow this statement in his paper book; but what that meant I knew not.

"Your father and mother?" said he. "My father was Alexander Balfour," said I, "and my mother Grace Pitarrow."

"Have you any papers proving your identity?" asked Mr. Rankeillor.

"No, sir," said I, "but they are in the hands of Mr. Campbell. Mr. Campbell, too, would give me his word; and for that matter, I do not think my uncle would deny me."

"Meaning Mr. Ebenezer Balfour?" said he.

"The same," said I.

"Did you ever meet a man of the name of Hoseason?" asked Mr. Rankeillor.

"I did so, sir, for my sins," said I; "for it was by his means and the procurement of my uncle, that I was kidnapped, carried to sea, suffered shipwreck and a hundred other hardships, and stand before you today in this poor garb."

"You say you were shipwrecked," said Rankeillor; "where was that?"

"Off the south end of the Isle of Mull," said I. "The name of the isle on which I was cast up is the Island Earraid."

"Ah!" he exclaimed. But so far, I may tell you, this agrees pretty exactly with other information that I hold. However, the ship was lost on June the 27th, and we are now at August the 24th. Here is a considerable hiatus, of nearly two months. It has already caused a vast amount of trouble to your friends; and I own I shall not be very well contented until it is set right."

"Indeed, sir," said I, "these months are very

easily filled up; but yet before I told my story, I would be glad to know that I was talking to a friend."

"This is to argue in a circle," said the lawyer. "I cannot be convinced till I have heard you. I cannot be your friend till I am properly informed."

"You are not to forget, sir," said I, "that I have already suffered by my trustfulness, and was shipped off to be a slave by the very man that is your employer".

At this sally, which I made with something of a smile myself, he laughed aloud.

"No," said he, "it is not as bad as that. I was indeed your uncle's man of business; but while you were gallivanting in the west, a good deal of water has run under the bridges; and if your ears did not sing, it was not for lack of being talked about. On the very day of your sea disaster, Mr. Campbell stalked into my office, demanding you from all the winds. I had never heard of your existence, but I had known your father; and from matters in my competence I was disposed to fear the worst."

"Mr. Ebenezer admitted having seen you and declared that he had given you considerable sums, and that you had started for Europe, intending to fulfill your education. I am not exactly sure that anyone believed him," Mr. Rankeillor added.

"Then Captain Hoseason came up with the story of your drowning; upon which all fell through, with no consequence other than causing grief and anxiety to Mr. Campbell, injury to my pocket, and another blot upon your uncle's character, which he could ill afford."

"And now, Mr. Balfour," said he, "you understand the whole process of these matters, and can judge for yourself to what extent I may be trusted."

"Sir," said I, "if I tell you my story, I must commit a friend's life to your discretion. Pass me your word it shall be sacred; and for what touches myself, I will ask no better guarantee than just your face."

He passed me his word very seriously.

"But if there are in your story any little jostles to the law," said he, "I would beg you to bear in mind that I am a lawyer."

Thereupon, I told him my story from the first.

But when I mentioned the name of Alan Breck, we had an odd scene. The name of Alan had of course rung through Scotland, with the news of the Appin murder.

"I would take no unnecessary names, Mr. Balfour," said Rankeillor; "above all, of Highlanders, many of whom are hateful to the law."

"Well, it might have been better not," said I, "but since I have let it slip, I may as well continue."

"Not at all," said Mr. Rankeillor. "I am somewhat dull of hearing, as you may have remarked; and I am far from sure I caught the name exactly. We will call your friend, if you please, Mr. Thomson, so that there may be no reflections. And in future, I would take some such way with any Highlander that you may have to mention -- dead or alive."

By this, I saw he must have heard the name all too clearly, and had already guessed I might be coming to the murder. Through all the rest of my story Alan was Mr. Thomson. James Stewart, in like manner, was mentioned under the style of Mr. Thomson's kinsman; Colin Campbell passed as a Mr. Glen.

"Well, well," said the lawyer, when I had quite done, "this is a great Odyssey of yours."

Mr. Rankeillor then invited me to dinner, gave me a change of clothes, and allowed me to wash.

CHAPTER 22

I Go in Quest of My Inheritance

When I had finished, Mr. Rankeillor called me again into the cabinet.

He gave me some information about my father and uncle. He was embarrassed to say that their problems had hinged on a love affair.

"Really," said I, "I cannot very well join that idea with my uncle."

"But your uncle, Mr. David, was not always

old," replied the lawyer, "and what may perhaps surprise you more, not always ugly. He had a fine, gallant air; people stood in their doors to look after him, as he went by upon a mettle horse.

Mr. Rankeillor recounted how the two brothers fell in love with the same woman. Ebenezer was confident of winning the girl because of his looks, but was mistaken. So, he sulked and whined to every neighbor he met. My father was a tender-hearted man and finally decided to let Ebenezer marry the girl. She, however, did not agree to their decision, as she had loved only my father.

So, my father made one concession after another to the selfish Ebenezer.

Finally, they agreed that Ebenezer would take the estate.

As a result, my parents were poor for the rest of their lives. Money was all that Ebenezer got by this bargain.

"Well, sir," said I, after thinking awhile about

what Mr. Rankeillor had just said, "and in all this, what is my position?"

"The estate is yours beyond a doubt," replied he. "It matters nothing what your father signed, you are the heir of entail. But your uncle is a man to fight the indefensible; and it would be likely your identity that he would call in question. A lawsuit is always expensive, and a family lawsuit always scandalous; besides which, if any of your doings with your friend Mr. Thomson were to come out, we might find ourselves in a false position. The kidnapping would be a court card upon our side, if we could only prove it. But it may be difficult to prove; and my advice is to make a very easy bargain with your uncle."

I told him I was willing to be easy. But I also began to think of a plan to trap the old man. We had to show Ebenezer the proof of the kidnapping out of court. So, I related my plan to Rankeillor.

Rankeillor was dismayed that he would have to meet Mr. Thomson; but, he said that he liked

the plan. After dinner, Rankeillor asked me many questions about the plan and then had his clerk, Torrance, record his notes officially.

When the clerk left, Rankeillor told me a story about a time when he forgot his glasses and could not recognize Torrance.

The clerk soon returned with the documents and a basket; and we set off to find Alan.

At last we were clear of the houses, and began

towards the Hawes Inn and the Ferry pier, the scene of my misfortune.

All of a sudden, Mr. Rankeillor cried out, clapped his hand to his pockets, and began to laugh.

"Why," he cried, "if this be not a farcical adventure! After all that I said, I have forgotten my glasses!"

I understood at once that if he had left his spectacles at home, it had been done on purpose, so that he might have the benefit of Alan's help, without the awkwardness of recognizing him.

And indeed it was well thought upon; for now how could Rankeillor swear to my friend's identity, or how be made to bear damaging evidence against myself?

As soon as we were past the Hawes, I went up the hill, whistling from time to time and at length I had the pleasure to hear it answered and to see Alan rise from behind a bush. I filled him in on all that had passed.

"And that is a very good notion of yours," said Alan, "and I dare to say that you could lay your hands upon no better man to put it through than Alan Breck."

Then I cried and waved on Mr. Rankeillor, who came up alone.

"Mr. Thomson, I am pleased to meet you," said Mr. Rankeillor. "But I have forgotten my glasses; and our friend, Mr. David here will tell you that I am little better than blind, and that you must not be surprised if I pass you by tomorrow."

Night had almost set in when we came in view of the house of Shaws.

As we drew near we saw no glimmer of light in any portion of the building. It seemed my uncle was already in bed. We made our last whispered consultations some fifty yards away; and then the lawyer, Torrance and I crouched down beside the corner of the house. As soon as we were in our places, Alan strode to the door and began to knock.

CHAPTER 23

I Come Into My Kingdom

Alan knocked loudly for a while before any movement could be heard. After a while, uncle Ebenezer opened a window.

"What's this?" said he. "What brings you here? I have a shot-gun."

"Is that you, Mr. Balfour?" returned Alan. "Careful about that shot-gun; they're nasty things to burst."

"What brings you here? And who are you?" said my uncle, angrily.

"I don't have the inclination to shout out my name," said Alan. "But what brings me here is more of your affair than mine; and if you like I'll set it to a tune and sing it to you."

"And what is it?" asked my uncle.

"David," said Alan.

"What!" cried my uncle, in a changed voice.

Then, after a while, he said, "I think I'd better let you in."

However, Alan refused, desiring to speak in front of us (who were hiding that time) so that Mr. Rankeillor could hear it from Ebenezer's own mouth.

Uncle Ebenezer was forced to come to the doorstep. He sat on the step, warning Alan again that he had a shot-gun.

"Now, tell your business," he told Alan.

Alan told my uncle how he and his friends had come upon me on the Isle of Mull, and had brought me to a castle thereon. Yet, since my staying was expensive, Alan threatened that Ebenezer would never see me again if he did not pay a ransom.

My uncle cleared his throat.

"I don't care much," said he. "He wasn't a good lad, and I've no need to interfere. I'll pay no ransom, and you can what you like with him."

"Hoot, sir," says Alan. "Blood's thicker than water! You cannot desert your brother's son; and if you did, and it came out, you wouldn't be very popular in your country-side."

"I'm not very popular even now," returned Ebenezer.

"No?" said Alan. "Well, see here: if you don't want the lad back, what do you want done with him, and how much will you pay for it?"

My uncle made no answer, but shifted uneasily on his seat.

"Come, sir," said Alan, "I ask for nothing but plain dealing. In two words: do you want the lad killed or kept?"

"O, sirs!" cried Ebenezer. "O, sirs, me! That's no kind of language!"

"Killed or kept?" repeated Alan.

"O, kept, kept!" wailed my uncle.

"Well," said Alan, "as you please; now what about the price? For instance, what you gave Hoseason during the first time?"

"Hoseason!" cried my uncle, struck aback. "What for?"

"For kidnapping David," says Alan.

"It's a lie, it's a black lie!" cried my uncle. "He was never kidnapped."

"That's no fault of mine or yours," said Alan; "but, you see, Hoseason is not a man that can be trusted. He has told me everything. He and I are partners now."

"Well," said my uncle, "I don't care what he said. He lied, and the solemn truth is this, that I gave him twenty pounds. But I'll be perfectly honest with you: he was to sell the lad in Carolina,

and get the money for that as well."

"Thank you, Mr. Thomson. That will do excellently well," said the lawyer, stepping forward.

And then, mighty civilly, he said, "Good-evening, Mr. Balfour."

"And good-evening, Uncle Ebenezer," said I.

My uncle never said a word; but just sat where he was on the top door-step and stared upon us.

Alan filched away his shotgun, and the lawyer, taking him by the arm, led him into the kitchen. We all followed, and set him down in a chair beside the hearth.

There we all looked upon him for a while, exulting greatly in our success, but yet with a sort of pity for the man's shame.

"Come Mr. Ebenezer," said the lawyer, "you must not be down-hearted, for I promise you we shall make easy terms. In the meanwhile give us the cellar key, and Torrance shall draw us a bottle of your father's wine."

Then, turning to me and taking me by the hand, "Mr. David," said he, "I wish you all joy in your good fortune."

And then to Alan, "Mr. Thomson, I pay you my compliment; it was most artfully conducted."

By that time we had the fire lighted, and a bottle of wine uncorked; a good supper came out of the basket. Torrance, Alan and I sat down to the meal, while the lawyer and my uncle went into the next chamber to consult. They stayed there for about an hour at the end of which period they had come to a good understanding.

By the terms of this, my uncle made Rankeillor agree to pay me two clear thirds of the yearly income of Shaws.

So the beggar in the ballad had come home; and when I lay down that night on the kitchen chests, I was a man of wealth and had a name in the country.

I lay till dawn, looking at the roof and planning the future.

Though the future was looking bright for me, I still wondered what I should do with Alan and what he might do for James of the Glens.

I spoke to Mr. Rankeillor about these issues the next morning. He felt that I was bound to help Mr. Thomson, but doubted that I should endanger myself in the case of James. My testimony to a Highland court would not be given much credence, he reasoned.

Then we hurried inside so that Mr. Rankeillor could write two letters for me. One letter was signed to the British Linen Company, a bank, to give me credit. The second letter was for the lawyer, Mr. Balfour of Pilrig, who could represent me to the advocate in the murder case.

Thereupon he took his farewell, and set out with Torrance, while Alan and I turned our faces for the city of Edinburgh.

Walking along, Alan and I had difficulty in speaking to each other as we knew that we would have to part soon. We tried discussing our plans for the upcoming days. Alan would hide about the country, coming once daily to a singular spot where I or a messenger could find him. I would seek out a lawyer who was an Appin Stewart and who could thus find a ship for Alan's departure.

Soon, we reached a spot looking over the city called Rest-and-be-Thankful.

We both stopped, for, we both knew that

we had come to where our ways parted. Here I gave Alan what money I had (a guinea or two of Rankeillor's) so that he should not starve in the meanwhile; and then we stood and looked over at Edinburgh in silence.

"Well, good-bye," said Alan, and held out his left hand. "Good-bye," said I, and gave the hand a little grasp, and went off down hill.

As I went on my way to the city, I felt so lost and lonesome, that I would have liked to sit down by the dyke, and cry and weep like any baby. It was nearly noon when I passed in by the West Kirk and the Grassmarket into the busy streets of the capital.

Lost in my thoughts I let the crowd carry me to and fro; and all the time what I was thinking of was Alan at Rest-and-be-Thankful. The hand of Providence brought me in my drifting to the very doors of the British Linen Company's bank.

The End